*A
Harlequin
Romance*

THE SILENT MOON

by

JAN ANDERSEN

HARLEQUIN BOOKS

Toronto • Canada   New York • New York

THE SILENT MOON

First published in 1971 by Mills & Boon Limited,
17 - 19 Foley Street, London, England

Harlequin Canadian edition published June, 1971
Harlequin U.S. edition published September, 1971

Standard Book Number: 373-51499-9.

Printed in Canada

CHAPTER ONE

THE letter came on a Saturday morning, which was just as well since it was the only time the three Frasers could be quite certain of being together. It was addressed to Alan, but Jo saw it first and pounced because of the South African stamp. Sally, the wise one, withdrew it gently.

"It's for Alan, not you. And anyway, I thought you said you didn't care one way or the other whether you ever heard from him again."

Jo moved uneasily. "I don't. No—that's not strictly true, I would like to know what happened to him, whether he made his fortune."

"Bruce Farley will never make his fortune . . . No, I'm sorry Jo, that's not quite fair," Sally added, quickly repentant as her sister's colour deepened. "He *was* rather super, I agree. But not exactly the settling down type."

"An adventurer, I think was your word for him," Jo said coldly. She had got up and was standing at the window as if engrossed in something outside. Only the quick nervous movement of her fingers rolling the blind cord gave her away. "Anyway, who said anything about settling down? Bruce is a prospector, not a bank clerk. He wasn't likely to stay digging for diamonds in Derbyshire, was he?"

"I'm sorry, Jo," Sally caught the edge to her sister's voice and cursed herself for her thoughtlessness. "Of course not. But it just hurts me to see you hurt, that's all."

"*Bruce did not hurt me.*" Jo's voice was so tense now Sally knew she had only made it worse. "We liked each

5

other, that's all. And then he went away. The fact that he's no good at writing letters is not . . ."

"Good God!"

Both sisters swung towards their brother. The first words he had spoken—and strong words for him. He had reached the bulky South African envelope and tipped its contents on to the breakfast table. They stared at the two airline tickets lying there.

"Who are they for?" Jo breathed. "You?"

Alan shook his head. "There are no names. But they can't be for me—and anyway, why two?"

Jo reached over and grabbed. "You must have gone in for a competition or something." She flipped through the pages, adding ominously. "They're singles."

From the floor, where the other mail had slipped, unheeded, Sally retrieved a typed airmail letter. "*This* might tell you. Read it," she commanded, "I can't bear the suspense any longer."

As Alan read the closely packed page his eyebrows seemed to rise higher and higher. But the only words he spoke were: "Uncle *Harold*! I thought he'd died years ago."

"And now I suppose," Jo put in dramatically, "we're suddenly heirs to a huge fortune."

Alan did not answer until he reached the end of the letter and then he said slowly, as if she had just made the statement, "Well, I don't know about a fortune, but we are his heirs—at least I think we are."

"Tell us," Sally said, "by the time we've all read the letter lunch time will be here."

Alan pushed his hair back from his forehead. "Well, I'll try, if I can decode the legal language. It seems that Uncle Harold has just died and he's so out of touch he thinks there's just you and me, Sally. His only asset is a small game park called Nyala on the . . . in one of the countries bordering on South Africa. Get a map, please, someone."

6

"And he's left it to us . . . you?" Jo put in.

"I suppose he has, but with strings. As far as I can gather the Government wants to take it over as it's one of the few private reserves left. Finances are precarious, but he wanted to keep it in the family. If we can show we could make the place pay, then in three months the park is ours. If not, the Government has it. Hence the tickets. I think that's the gist of it, but you can read the letter if you like, Sally."

Jo said thoughtfully, "I didn't even know there was an Uncle Harold. And what was he doing in South Africa anyway?"

"I'm not really sure," Alan replied. "I know there was some kind of blazing family row and he went there after the war. I must have been three or four and Sally just a baby. As there's no mention of you, Jo, he couldn't have even known you were born. He was Dad's younger brother, but why there should have been this complete break beats me."

"And why should we be his heirs?" Sally put in. "Didn't he marry or anything? People don't usually leave everything to a niece and nephew they haven't seen for twenty years. It strikes me as being very fishy."

But Jo's mind had jumped a few paces. "Where did you say this place . . . this park is? Have we got an atlas, Alan?"

"Yes, on top of the cupboard there, but I don't see . . ."

Jo reached the atlas down and opened it at the right page. "Now, do you remember that South African you brought home for a meal from the hotel last year, Alan? Mr. . . ."

"Brand. Neil Brand. But what's he got to do with it?"

"Think back, Alan," she said eagerly. "You couldn't understand why he had chosen a small village in the North of England for a stay. And he was terribly anxious

7

to meet Sally and to see our home. Where did he come from?"

"I'm not sure exactly, but it was somewhere in this area."

"All those questions he asked," Sally put in, "you mean you think Uncle Harold asked him to come and look us over?"

Jo shrugged. "Well, it's possible, isn't it? Although it doesn't explain why I've been left out. Perhaps he didn't like me ... I must say he seemed to take a fancy to you, Sal."

Alan suddenly folded the letter. "O.K., so that's one bit of the mystery solved, but it's not going to do us much good. The game park isn't ours until we've made it pay, and since we can't do that the whole thing is a waste of time even thinking about."

"And the tickets?" Jo put in hopefully.

"Send them back, I suppose. They're only singles, so we can't go and have a cheap holiday. We'd have to find about three hundred pounds to get back. In any case I couldn't get off for three weeks, much less three months." He glanced at his watch. "Heavens, I must fly. I've an appointment at eleven."

"Will you be back for lunch?" Usually it was Sally who asked the practical questions, but this time it was Jo, who could barely keep the suppressed excitement from her voice.

"About one-thirty," he called, "but don't wait for me."

When he had gone, Sally looked at her younger sister. "Come on, out with it, I can tell you've got some crazy scheme up your sleeve. We'll do the washing up later."

Jo sat down again. "All right, I've got a scheme, but I don't think it's crazy, and you must hear me through and think hard before you condemn it."

Sally went out to get her hair done. It was Jo's turn to stay at home and do the Saturday chores. For once she was quite glad to be on her own and think things out a little more clearly. The Frasers, she had decided this morning, were getting into a rut.

They had always been a close-knit family, so when their parents were killed just five years ago, the three of them decided to stick together and keep on the house they had lived in almost all their lives. Jo was in her last year at school and though she badly wanted to leave and take her share of the family finances she was persuaded that a better education would help them all. Sally was already at domestic science college and it seemed equally important that she should finish her training.

That first year was very hard, for although there was no mortgage on the house there was also no more than a few hundred pounds capital. Alan was doing the job he had wanted to ever since he was about fifteen—working his way up in a hotel business. But he was only twenty-two and still on a low salary. They managed somehow, with his working overtime, Sally doing private cooking in the evenings and Jo helping in the local supermarket every Saturday.

On the whole, Jo decided, it had been a good life, but now seemed the time for a change. It was time, for instance, that Sally, at twenty-four, thought a little of her own future instead of Alan's. She was rarely short of escorts and invitations, but there had never been anyone she had felt deeply enough about to give up the even, sunny pattern of her days. She loved the wild, bleak Derbyshire hills and dales that encircled the little town and nothing gave her greater pleasure than to roam the countryside for hours at a time seeking to extend her considerable collection of wild flowers.

And Jo herself? She could not really have said what she wanted from life. But she had turned twenty-one just two months ago and felt the same restless feeling overtaking her that had come with the departure of Bruce Farley. Only to herself could she admit that the ripples of his coming and going had never died.

9

It had been decided that she should put her idea to Alan. She knew she had not won her sister over completely, but Sally was wavering. And since they had always been a family to decide important issues by discussion she felt that Alan's reaction was of vital importance.

Jo managed to contain herself until Sally cleared away the table and brought in the coffee.

Alan stretched. "Have you two got plans for the rest of the day? I'd like the car for the evening if that's possible. I look like working late. But first I need some air."

"First," Jo said dramatically, "Sally and I have something to say to you."

He groaned. "I might have guessed you'd been thinking about those tickets all the morning. If you're thinking we can flog them, then you're very much mistaken."

Jo tossed her fine silky hair over her shoulders. "Don't jump to conclusions, Alan. First answer me one question. What is your greatest ambition?"

He frowned. "You know damn well what it is."

"You could have changed since last week. Go on, tell me."

As if he were humouring a child he answered: "To buy the Crag Inn."

"I heard that it really might come on to the market at the end of the year."

"You've only heard what the whole town has heard. Are you proposing, my dear little sister, to write me out a cheque for the twenty thousand pounds that I need so badly?"

"Not exactly, but . . ."

"Then do me a favour and shut up about it. Even talk sets all my nerves a-quiver."

"All right, Alan, I'll come to the point, but I'll say the same to you as I did to Sally. Don't interrupt until I've finished.

"You said this morning you can't take three months

off because you have a living to earn. All right, fair enough. Being manager of the Crown is the next best thing to owning the Crag, so you don't want to lose that job."

"Jo, for heaven's sake . . . !"

"No, please, Alan, let me finish. But there's nothing to stop Sally and me taking the time off. I can get a secretarial job anywhere when I come back and I daresay Sally can get a catering one. You could move into the Crown and we could let the house for three months. If—and I know the if is a huge gamble—Sally and I could just keep this park's head above water for three months, then it's ours, or rather yours. You could then sell it and buy the Crag."

Alan turned to stare at her and she felt a queer little twist of triumph. She could see at least she had caught his attention.

"But you two haven't the faintest idea how to run a game park. You've never even seen one."

"Of course not. But there must be someone there doing it now. Anyway, it's only small. What do you suppose that means—twenty or thirty acres?"

"If it's that small, you wouldn't get twenty thousand pounds for it. I imagine a few hundred acres would be nearer the mark, but don't ask me. My experience of game is the odd elephant and lion I've seen at the zoo. Anyway, it's an insane idea. If the finances are as precarious as this letter indicates, how do you think you're going to do any better than Uncle Harold, or his manager?"

"I don't think at all," Jo said calmly, "I just know it's worth a gamble."

"A gamble that could cost you more than three hundred pounds," he said with heavy sarcasm.

It was Sally who came to the rescue in her quiet way.

"Look, Alan, I too thought it was crazy this morning, but I've sat under the hair-drier thinking about nothing else, and at least I don't think we need lose. I agree with you that we may not save the park for ourselves, but it's worth a try. It's the only way you'll ever get that hotel, you know. The bank's never going to lend you the money. And once the Crag has slipped from the old ladies' hands into someone else's, then you've lost it for good. And this three hundred pounds? Well, I've thought about that too. Personally I don't think the solicitors could leave us stranded there without return tickets, if we *are* forced to leave. But in any case, if things are bad we should recognise it pretty early. One of us will just have to go to work. I may not be able to earn three hundred pounds in three months, but I daresay I could manage half. So we've spent as much as a good holiday for two."

Jo's heart gave a great lift of joy. With Sally on her side, Alan would at least listen. Actually, if it came to that, he could hardly stop them.

He had got up from the table and was pacing the room. "I don't know; I just don't know, I feel so responsible."

"We are," Sally reminded him gently, "both over age."

"I know, but neither of you has ever been farther than Spain. Heaven knows what the climate's like. I suppose you, Jo, think you might run into Bruce Farley."

Her head shot up in anger. "That's a rotten remark, Alan! I hadn't given him a thought. And in case you hadn't realised it, Africa is a large continent, not a one-eyed hole like this."

"I'm sorry, Jo, I wasn't thinking. You really are thinking of me, aren't you?"

Jo smiled. "You're the only one with ambition. Besides, I've rather fancied living up at the Crag too, and if I have to sit three months in the sun to do it, well, who's grumbling?"

"Well, I don't know, it seems pretty crazy—" He

turned finally to Sally. "It really rests with you, Sal, since Jo isn't mentioned in the will. I'd have to give you power of attorney or something."

"I'm quite sure, Alan," she said. "I don't think we've got much hope, but it's worth it. Can you imagine Mother and Dad hesitating when so much is at stake?"

He shook his head. "No. No, I couldn't." He reached into his pocket and once more brought out the tickets. "Three weeks today. It's not long, is it? I shall miss you both."

They sat and talked about it until they could talk no more. Then, as Jo made fresh coffee, Sally suddenly disappeared. She came down ten minutes later, her face dusty, her arms full of books.

"Where on earth did you get those?" Alan asked. He took them from her. All were old, with dust jackets torn or disappeared.

"How extraordinary!" He opened them one by one. "Two Stuart Cloete novels, four travel books, one about the early diamond days, a biography of Cecil Rhodes, even this, about the Kruger Park. They're *all* about South Africa." He looked across at his sister questioningly.

"Do you remember when Mother and Dad died and we had to go through all their personal things? Well, there was this trunk belonging to Mother in the attic. It had her wedding dress in it, those old party invitations, all the odd special things she had treasured. And we decided to keep it, didn't we?"

"That's right," Alan said, "only I think I left it all to you."

"Well, these books were at the bottom. I've never thought of them until this moment. Why aren't they on the bookshelves? And why are they all about South Africa? Mother has never been there. Did she have other friends or relatives?"

"I never heard of anyone but Uncle Harold. Put them

on the shelves, Sally. You . . . you'll probably both want to dip into them."

Jo started to gather up the cups. There were the beginnings of another mystery here, but one that made her feel faintly uneasy—and one they might never be able to unravel. Very loudly she said, "Well, I shall start on the one about the Kruger Park, we should be able to pick up some tips from that." And then a few moments later : "For both your benefits, the nyala is a kind of antelope, timid and strikingly beautiful. It lives in bush covered regions near the water, and feeds on leaves, young roots and wild fruits." She grinned mischievously. "I think I'm going to like Nyala."

CHAPTER TWO

IT was mid-afternoon, just three weeks later, when the jet circled the vast Transvaal plateau and came down with a hiss of wheels on the runway of Jan Smuts Airport.

On the tarmac Jo breathed deeply of the warm, scented air and turned to her sister. "Well, we really are here, aren't we?"

Sally seemed to shake her head. "I think so. I can't be sure of anything this last week, except that I've learned you're a very forceful organiser."

Jo grinned. "For those few kind words, many thanks."

Little more than half an hour later a taxi was dropping them outside their hotel in the centre of Johannesburg, a noisy throbbing city of straight roads and high, square buildings. But as they had driven through the suburbs the avenues lined with glorious purple jacaranda made them think they were entering paradise.

The tiredness that had been building up through excitement and worry during the past week hit them almost as soon as they had eaten, and they slept for twelve hours, to wake and realise the main part of their journey was about to begin. But before they went to the airport again they had to see the solicitor.

They did not learn very much more than through the letter. Harold Fraser had made his will several years ago, but it was only in the last few months that he had added the codicil about the game park's ownership.

At one point Jo asked curiously: "Do you think he knew of my existence?"

"Not as far as I know, Miss Fraser. To be honest I knew very little indeed about Mr. Harold Fraser. He was my client and I dealt with his business affairs, but about his private life I knew almost nothing."

"He never married?"

"No, I believe he was a very solitary sort of person. That's probably why the life out at Nyala suited him. Oh, yes, I did know one thing about him. He had a passionate interest in the Bushmen and I believe spent any spare time out in the Kalahari studying their ways and their history."

Jo had one more question to ask. "Mr. Scott, we very nearly didn't come because we thought if we failed to make the park pay then we shouldn't be able to afford the money for our return tickets. If . . . if the Government does buy, who has the money?"

He smiled. "First, Miss Fraser, you need have no worries about returning to England. That will be taken care of. But if you should not succeed in your uncle's wish, then I'm afraid there will be no money. The Government will be able to claim Nyala. A strange legacy, you may think, but then your uncle was a strange man. As I say I knew very little about him except he was what in modern idiom is known as a lone wolf. I suspect there was some disappointment in his life, but unlike others in the same position he did not seek revenge, rather atonement. That is why, I imagine, he felt he did not want to make capital out of this game reserve he had been building up with such loving care over twenty years. And the task he set himself could not have been an easy one. It's a forbidding part of the country to live in and it must have taken a great deal of courage for an Englishman to come to terms with it."

Sally smiled faintly. "Are you warning us, Mr. Scott?"

"No, I don't think so, Miss Fraser, I'm a legal man and I can only go on facts. I think your hopes of success are slender, partly because of the financial difficulties and partly because you know nothing of the climate or terrain. Up there nature can be very cruel. And yet I hope and pray for your success, because I feel strongly that your uncle would like the land to stay in the family—unless of course the Government does take it over, compulsorily. Most game parks have been nationalised, you know."

"Did Uncle Harold ever ask a subsidy from the Government?" Sally asked thoughtfully.

"I don't know, but I doubt it, for the very good reason that he would have to seek legal advice before taking a step like that. And you know he was a very proud and independent man. I feel it would have been a final step for him."

He glanced at his watch. "And now, regretfully, young ladies, I shall have to remind you that your plane leaves in just over the hour. I can only wish you luck and emphasise that I am here to help you whenever you need me. Do you know anyone, or have you any friends in South Africa?"

Both girls shook their heads.

"Then we must really make sure of having a meeting somewhere near half way through your term."

"You could come for a weekend perhaps, Mr. Scott?" Sally put in hopefully.

"It might be the best, then I could see things for myself. But I believe you have an excellent manager—or warden as he would be known up there. A Mr. Ross Andrews."

"You know him?"

"Alas, no, but he has been with your uncle nearly four years, so he must be satisfactory."

He bade them goodbye and once more they were on their way to the airport.

In the taxi Jo turned to Sally. "Did you think what I did?"

Sally nodded. "I imagine so. When he mentioned about no money changing hands and Uncle not wanting to make capital out of the Park? If he had only known that all we want to do is to sell . . ."

"Well," returned Jo firmly, "it's no good feeling guilty or sentimental. It's what we've come out here to do. It's not even as if we knew Uncle Harold. And I imagine neither of us wants to spend our life up on the edge of the desert with no one but lions and snakes for company."

"Oh," said Sally in a small voice. "I'd thought of lions, but not of snakes. Do you think there'll be many?"

"There always are in deserts, aren't there? I've only read about Kruger, so everything is guesswork."

An hour later they were airborne, but this time in a small plane that held only a dozen passengers. Word must have got round as to who they were, for the young pilot insisted they took the two front seats so he could point out some of the interesting points in the landscape.

The plane landed first at the capital, a small dusty town just over the border. Six of the passengers left the plane and two more joined it. When the pilot took off again for the last leg of the flight north he said over his shoulder: "Now you'll see a bit of the real country. Look out of the port window."

Jo strained her eyes into the endless distance. "It's not like a country at all, more like a great wasteland."

"The original tribes called it the Thirstland. Now there are only the Bushmen left, and they have to struggle even to exist. You can travel for days in the desert without even the scent of water."

"Is . . . is it like that where we're going?" Sally said cautiously.

"It's tough enough, but you're only on the edge. I believe part of the Nyala Reserve is very beautiful. Only the far side of it touches the real desert. But I wouldn't know except from the air. Your uncle . . . he was your uncle, wasn't he? . . . didn't encourage visitors."

"But . . ." The question died on Jo's lips. This man was not the one to ask. Undoubtedly his knowledge of Nyala was only based on gossip and rumour.

Once or twice he took the small plane low, to swoop over a river or to show one of the rough tracks across the desert, or the area where the best game gathered.

Just before they finally landed he said in his broad accent : "Well, girls, if you get tired of the wild life, send me a message and I'll give you both a night on the town. And I mean that. Not many pretty girls up in this part of the world. I have to look for my social life down in Jo'burg. And I reckon *you* won't be seeing much social life. They do say that Andrews has picked up some of the old man's ways." On that faintly uncomfortable note he brought the wheels down on to the runway of an airstrip that seemed no more than a cluster of huts at one end of a brown baked field.

Outside, it was like walking into a thick wall of heat. Even the airport building was hardly cooler and there was not a white face to be seen.

Sally clutched Jo's arm. "Do you think we were mad after all?"

Jo shrugged. "Probably. But now I know we've at least got our air passage back, I'm going to stick it out. I've been alive for twenty-one years and I've never had a real adventure."

Sally smiled her gentle smile. "Sometimes I think you should have been the elder sister. We might have made our fortunes by now."

"Silly!" Jo squeezed her arm, "someone's got to keep my feet on the ground, and I'd sooner it was you. Now, do you suppose we're expected, or do we just hail a taxi and drive into the bush?"

Even as she spoke a tall African in old but beautifully pressed khaki trousers and shirt came from the shadows of the hall, bowed briefly and handed them a letter.

"*Morena* send this, ladies."

Sally opened the letter. It was short and to the point. "Sorry I couldn't meet you. Kari is my right-hand man and will drive you safely to Nyala. Make sure you bring

19

with you the following items, particularly those from the chemist."

Sally handed the list to Jo. "He must think we're going to get every disease in the book! The rest—well, I suppose he knows what he's talking about."

When they had shopped, Kari escorted them to the hotel for lunch and told them he would collect them in one hour to drive them to Nyalá.

"Is it a long drive?" Sally asked.

"Not long, lady."

But Kari's idea of 'not long' and their own seemed to be very different. At the end of each hour one of them would ask: "Is it far now?" And he would shake his head and repeat cheerfully, "Not far now." And the truck would go rumbling on over the hot, dusty road.

The farther north they drove, the more oppressive seemed to grow the heat. To open the window only invited the flying dust. On either side of the road was nothing but endless bush, scrub and thorn. Then they would come to a kind of village, a group of huts and smiling black children waving as they passed. Finally Kari had to stop for petrol and Jo said firmly: "We must have some water. My sister is not feeling well."

He looked behind dubiously and from a basket in the back produced a vacuum flask. Jo could only hope that the warmish water it contained was fresh, but at that moment she did not particularly care. Sally looked all in. Then Kari came back carrying two oranges and handed them to them in some triumph.

"Good for the ladies."

"Thank you," said Jo, "but please, we have been driving for four hours. You must tell us how far it is now."

"Not far, lady," came the now familiar answer.

"I want to know exactly how far," Jo said inexorably. She pointed to her watch.

"One hour. That is all."

Inevitably it turned out to be two, for shortly after the

20

stop for petrol they turned off the 'main' road on to one that in England would have been called little more than a farm track.

By now Sally looked thoroughly ill. All the colour had left her cheeks and she was lying back against the window with her eyes closed.

"Would you like to stop for a while, Sal?" Jo asked, when she realised that the continual bumping of the truck was driving her sister beyond endurance.

Sally looked out of the window. There was practically no shade and even where there was, the temperature was probably not far off a hundred.

She tried to smile. "I think I'll try to stick it out. I'd forgotten what a rotten traveller I am."

Kari glanced across anxiously. "Soon, lady, soon." And sure enough in less than half an hour he was pointing to a border of tall trees. "That is the river. On the other side of the river is Nyala."

"Thank God!"

Quite abruptly the country became green again, as if rain had recently washed the thorn and the scrubby bushes. And then they crossed the river on a narrow log bridge and started up another track running parallel to it. But there was no chance to see more because the swift tropical night came down without warning and the only way they knew they had arrived was by the gleam of lights through the darkness.

Stiffly Jo climbed down from the truck and reached up a hand to help her sister. "It's all right, Sal, we really are there, and it seems quite civilised."

But Sally was past caring. It was as much as she could do to walk up a few steps of the bungalow, across the verandah and into the large sitting room.

Jo pushed her gently into the low basket chair. "You'll feel tons better when you've had a cool drink. I'll ask Kari..."

But Kari had already gone ahead and within a

surprisingly short time had produced tall glasses of some mysterious fruit drink piled high with ice.

As Sally reached thankfully for her glass a voice behind her, sharp with command, said, "Don't touch that!" And then: "Kari, take this away. You know what I've told you about visitors." And the two inviting glasses were whisked away.

Jo looked across towards the man who had just come in through the open door. A lean man with muscles like whipcord, weathered skin almost the colour of copper and cool grey eyes that seemed to hold a faintly unwelcoming look.

Jo met that look with one of anger. "Is your opinion of visitors *that* low? Hundreds of miles across a stifling desert and we aren't even allowed a drink?"

He looked from Jo to Sally. "To the first part of your question Miss Fraser, I'm not over-keen on visitors, but once they are an established fact I don't want to act as nursemaid to them. I have enough on my plate."

"So—no drinks!"

"No ice," he corrected, as the drinks were brought in again in fresh glasses. "God knows what damage it could do to your sister in the dehydrated state she's in." He came farther into the room and watched for a moment while they drank, then ordered more. He held out a hand. "I'm Ross Andrews. I won't ask if you've had a good journey because it would be an impossible feat without an air-conditioned car."

In the same cool tone Jo replied, "I'm Jo Fraser, and this is my sister Sally."

"I was told a brother and sister were coming."

"No, Alan couldn't get away."

"I see." He eyed them both speculatively. "Have you ever been to Africa before?"

"No." Jo shook her head.

"Well then, you two should be just the people needed to set Nyala on its feet."

Jo stared, appalled, at this taut, sarcastic man. She had not given much thought to the man behind the name of Ross Andrews, except that he had worked for her uncle for four years, so must have some feeling for Nyala. That she and Sally would be quite so unwelcome had not entered her head. Even now she could not begin to imagine why.

From beside her Sally, always quick to sense an atmosphere, said quietly, in an attempt to change the mood, "Is it always as hot as this, Mr. Andrews?"

"Usually. Did you really expect something like an English summer day?"

Sally flushed at his continued sarcasm, but Jo was already racing in like a young tiger. "Are you always so abominably rude without reason, Mr. Andrews? We didn't ask our uncle to make such a ridiculous will. We didn't ask the solicitor to send the air tickets. I realise you must have lost almost complete touch with civilisation living here, but haven't you enough sense left to see that my sister is not just hot and thirsty, but ill? If there's a bedroom for us, then perhaps we could go to it!"

He seemed about to say something, then, with barely altered expression, he opened the door and called something incomprehensible. A few minutes later an African appeared.

"This is Saku," Ross Andrews said, "he's my house servant and will see that you have everything you want. I usually have dinner about eight-thirty if you feel like joining me." He turned on his heel and walked out into the darkness.

It was just about the last thing Jo felt like doing; her anger went on simmering all the time she bathed and changed and helped Sally into bed.

Her sister did look a little better now, but she was too limp and exhausted to do anything more than lie on the rather spartan-looking bed.

"Can I get anything for you, Sal?" Jo said

softly. "Do you think I should try to find a doctor?"

"Out here?" That even brought a smile to Sally's lips.

"No, I think he's probably right. I'm suffering from some kind of heat exhaustion. I just want to sleep until morning. If you could just see that there's a fair supply of that fruit drink..." Her voice tailed off. She was almost asleep already.

Jo went back and examined her own small room, a twin of Sally's. Presumably Ross Andrews really had been expecting brother and sister. It was small, whitewashed and the simple furniture carved and unpainted. The only gesture to comfort was a zebra skin that covered a fair part of the bare stone floor. One thing was fairly certain, whatever few visitors came to Nyala, they were not women.

She would have liked to avoid a further meeting with Ross Andrews that night, but there seemed no point in postponement. There was little enough time to establish some kind of working relationship. Besides, now that she felt greatly refreshed, hunger drove her into the living room.

Hardly had she walked across to the window when Saku was by her side with a drink, saying in the curiously soft, lilting voice: "*Morena* here soon, lady. You sit." And he indicated the comfortable basket chair overlooking the garden.

The scent of the flowers was strong, and the sounds of the night were those she had never heard before, the insistent hum of crickets, like the soft orchestral background to the real music, an occasional great trumpeting roar that could only come from an elephant, a chorus of some other beast that seemed to come in on cue every few moments. She was suddenly intensely aware that these were the sounds of Africa she was hearing, that for mile upon mile a hundred different animals slept or prowled, awaiting the cool of the night to seek their prey.

She did not know what made her turn at that

moment—the sixth sense that tells one is not alone, for certainly there had been no sound. For just a second she thought the sinewy brown shape watching her from the corner of the room was a large dog, but almost immediately came the appalling realisation that she was face to face with her first lion that was not behind bars.

The animal did not move, but watched her steadfastly, making strange little sighing noises.

It was only afterwards that Jo was able to describe the feeling that was above all one of complete numbness. She did not even think of running—although there was simply nowhere to run—and the old saying that her limbs had turned to lead was the truest thing she knew. She could only wait for the inevitable, for she could not possibly imagine that a lion would come into a house unless it was very, very hungry. But in a curiously fatalistic way she could only hope he would get on with it soon.

She had not even cried out, the numbness was so great. The only movement along her entire body was the faint trickle of tears being squeezed from under her eyelids. But she was not even aware of that at the time.

It could have been five minutes or five hours that she sat there, her eyes never leaving the other huge liquid brown ones. So gentle, so friendly, she thought in a moment of fantasy.

Suddenly the spell was broken as the lion started to move. She closed her eyes and her body started to shake uncontrollably. But there was no slashing claw, no ghastly, suffocating death, only a heightening of the soft crooning noise, then a human voice speaking sharply, but quietly, "Goldie, out, out, out!"

When she opened her eyes at last, the lion was no longer there, but Ross Andrews was standing above her chair, a glass of brandy in his hand.

"Here," he said in a surprisingly gentle voice, "drink this."

But the lead was still in her limbs and the tears were racing silently down her cheeks. It was not until he took her head as if she were sick and forced the brandy between her lips that she finally focused on him. Then, as her teeth started to chatter, a rug was thrown round her shoulders.

All she could say was: "Did ... did you really hate us as much as all that, Mr. Andrews?"

He turned away from her. "My God, I'm not a monster! I wouldn't have had that happen for all the world. I can't begin to tell you ..."

To her enormous surprise she saw that his hands were clenched so tightly that she thought the joints must crack. So he did mind: he really did mind after all.

Somehow, suddenly, he was the one needing reassurance and she said, in a mild understatement, "It's all right, really it is, I haven't come to any harm. I simply did not know what to do, that's all. I've only ever seen one in a zoo."

"You did what only one person in a thousand would do, sit tight and not scream. I can only offer you an apology. I should have been here ten minutes ago, but I was held up by one of the usual problems that crop up around here. Tell me, Miss Fraser, you're obviously a brave young woman—are you also of the school that believes that the moment you fall off a horse you should remount immediately?"

"Yes ... yes, I think I am—in theory at least."

"Then sit there, turn around and don't move." He crossed to the open doorway and called gently, "Goldie—come!"

The lion padded back, crossed to Ross Andrews' side and rubbed herself against him, just as a large friendly dog would. In return he tickled her behind the ears.

"Up, Goldie," he commanded, and the great animal stood up on its hind legs and placed both front paws on

Andrews' shoulders, who then dived into his pocket and produced a banana. Very gently like a delicate cat, the lion took it from him. It was only then that Jo saw it was wearing a heavy leather collar.

"Now, go and lie down over there, Goldie, and not a sound out of you."

He poured himself a beer and came and sat down on the chair near Jo. "I found her as a cub nearly two years ago. She was the only survivor of the litter and had been deserted by the parents, although we found a dead lioness caught in a trap some days later that was probably the mother. Unlike what people think, most lions are easy to tame, and they're the gentlest, most playful creatures in the world and some of their instincts are almost human. Goldie knocked me down one day on the run and I think she really thought she had hurt me badly. She sat in a corner and snarled and spat, just like a child who refuses to admit it's done wrong, so sulks."

Jo found her voice at last. "Is it only you she knows? I mean, will she respond to strangers?"

"Oh, yes, although she won't play with anyone she doesn't know. And you have to make it quite clear who is master. To spoil a lion like a lap-dog is to invite contempt from it. Anyway, it's high time she went back to the bush and learned to fend for herself. I've just started taking her out on forays to teach her to hunt."

Jo, feeling her fear finally subside, decided she must take her lesson to its limits. "Will . . . will she let me touch her?"

"Of course. Goldie, come here."

The lioness padded across the room and stopped exactly between the two chairs. She turned those coppery eyes on Jo again and watched her with that earlier look of speculation.

"Behind the ears," Andrews said, "Just tickle her as you would a dog."

As Jo's fingers touched the rough, almost spiky coat, she simply could not believe that two days ago she was sitting in an English suburban house and now she was stroking a wild lion.

Andrews smiled dryly. "Now you're accepted. This is part of the day's ritual to her. She knows I eat at eight-thirty, and she's always here on the dot."

Like the huge dog she had first appeared to be Goldie padded to the far side of the room, stretched out and, seconds later, was snoring gently.

Ross Andrews turned back to Jo. "And your sister, how is she?"

"Asleep. I think she'll be all right tomorrow."

In a formal voice he went on: "I apologise for my apparent discourtesy when you arrived. My only excuse is that I've had rather a lot on my mind lately."

Jo watched him curiously, feeling the apology was only verbal; there was no real depth to it. She had not given very much thought to Ross Andrews, but her mental picture would have been of an older, more rugged, even seasoned man. This one could not have been much over thirty. There was a restlessness about him, as if even after a short while he found a house too confining.

When Saku indicated that the meal was ready, Ross Andrews stood up politely and waited for her to sit down.

"I'm afraid," he started, "you won't find London standards in our kitchen here. Your uncle only ever taught the boys what might be loosely described as bachelor cooking. We're big meat eaters and we get whatever fruit is in season."

"We don't come from London," Jo pointed out, "and we certainly didn't fly thousands of miles to find London standards. But there is one thing I would like to know."

"Yes?"

"Why do you find our presence here quite so irksome?

You thought highly of our uncle, I assume, or you wouldn't have stayed with him. Surely you must have had some inkling what was in his mind over his property?"

"None whatsoever. Your uncle and I worked very closely over running the reserve, but he never talked about his private affairs. In fact I didn't even know he had relatives in England until about a year ago. To be perfectly frank I always assumed he would hand over Nyala to the Parks Board. This is the only private game reserve of any size in the republic."

"But the solicitor said it was small. How many acres does it actually cover?"

"Acres, Miss Fraser?" He raised his eyebrows in faint amusement. "Nyala is about five hundred square miles."

"Five hundred square *miles*?" she repeated stupidly. "But . . . but that's as big as a whole county in England!"

"Of course. But out here it's nothing. And as far as big game parks go, the Gemsbok is four thousand square miles and the Kruger over seven thousand. Directly behind us lie a million square miles of desert. So space, acres, miles—they mean little."

Still stunned by the impact of this knowledge, Jo went on, "Mr. Andrews, does the name Neil Brand mean anything to you?"

"Yes, he's a farmer, one of your uncle's few close friends, as a matter of fact. I suppose you could call him a neighbour, although his property is about sixty miles from here. You know him?"

"We met him when he came to England, although he didn't mention Uncle Harold—in fact we didn't even know there was an Uncle Harold—he must have come to report back on us. That's probably why you never knew of us either." She paused. "You still haven't told me why you resent us here. You do, don't you?"

He shrugged. "This is not a place for women,

particularly for women who have no experience of the way of life here. It's tough, unforgiving, often unrewarding . . ."

Jo shook her head. "That's not your real reason, Mr. Andrews. *You* want this park to go to the Government, don't you?"

"Well, don't you think that would be much the best solution?" he challenged.

"For whom?"

"The animals, of course. You have simply no idea what it costs to try to keep this place running on a limited budget. In the state we're in at the moment, it only needs one good disaster—like the threatened drought—and we're finished, so is about a third of the game. I've given four years of my life to Nyala and I don't intend to see it ruined for the sake of a couple of girls who merely want to be able to say they own a game reserve in Africa!"

Quivering with anger now, Jo stood up and faced him. "How dare you throw these accusations at us, Mr. Andrews! You know nothing about us, and yet before we've been here more than a couple of hours you make accusations, you're rude and you think you can frighten us away with your pet lion. Oh yes, now I really do begin to believe you weren't so innocent in leaving me alone with Goldie. I think you would have enjoyed it if I'd lost my head and screamed the place down. Well, you won't get me or my sister out that way. I too can accuse. Perhaps you would like Nyala for yourself. Perhaps you expected my uncle to leave it to you!"

She had touched him on the raw at last. There were white spots of anger under that tanned skin. But, unlike her, he managed to control himself. Unhurriedly he pushed his plate aside, stood up and walked over to the open window. There, very deliberately, he lit a pipe before turning back towards her.

"At least, Miss Fraser, we know where we stand—on

opposite sides of the fence. Tell me, how do you propose to keep Nyala on its feet?"

"You know perfectly well I can't answer that question."

"All right, then let me ask another one. Supposing you do succeed, what are your plans at the end of three months?"

Jo swallowed. She never was very good at lying. But Sally was even worse, so it was just as well she wasn't here.

"I don't know that, either. You'll have to ask that question again at the end of a month."

"Oh, no, Miss Fraser, I won't be doing that—for the simple reason that I won't be here at the end of a month. If you intend to run Nyala, and you seem confident that you can, or you wouldn't have flown out here, then you and your sister must do it on your own. I'm leaving."

CHAPTER THREE

JO woke to the sound of birds, a morning song of piercing sweetness that made her think she was in England and the thrushes were nesting again. But she opened her eyes to her cell-like room at Nyala, the sun already burning in the sky, and sight of lemon tea on her bedside table.

Pulling her cotton robe round her, she went to the window, but her room was at the side of the house and she could see nothing but a dusty courtyard and the truck under its shelter of grass. Somewhere not far away was the sound of human voices babbling away in a strange tongue and, intermittently, the barking of a dog.

She took the tea into Sally's room. Her sister was awake, looking rather washed out, but a great deal more human than she did last night.

"Hello, Sal, you are better, aren't you? You had me worried."

"Yes, I'm all right, not exactly ready for a bush trek, but I daresay that will come tomorrow. I don't remember much about yesterday except that our host didn't seem too keen to see us."

"You can say that again. He even went as far as setting his pet lion on me."

"He did *what*?" Sally's eyes were filled with horror.

"Well, perhaps not deliberately, but he didn't quite get to dinner on time and left me to make my own acquaintance with the lion. Oh, she's apparently harmless enough, except that I didn't know it at the time. Anyway, Sal, we've got problems on our hands and a family conference is called for. I'm going to shower and dress. Shall I come back here?"

Sally shook her head. "No, it's too hot already. The sitting room looked as if it might be the coolest place."

As Jo came into the sitting room Saku padded behind her carrying a tray which he set out on a small table on the verandah. There was more tea, fresh mangoes, bread, and a bowl of wild honey.

For the first time Jo looked out towards the front of her new home. The long wooden bungalow was set in a semi-circle of trees overlooking an apron of short stubby grass. A kind of primitive hose snaked from the direction of the river and spurted occasional gouts of water on the grass. Towards the left there had even been an attempt at developing a shrubbery where poinsettias, purple oleander and sweet-smelling frangipani struggled to grow. There was no boundary to the garden; it just ended. Beyond, to one side, were the trees that bordered the river—she could just see the gleam of the water as it curved away from the house—but everywhere else was the bush, stretching as far as the eye could see.

From behind her Sally said, "It's both beautiful and frightening, isn't it? So vast."

"I know; and do you know one thing Ross Andrews told me last night? By some standards this might be a small game reserve, but not by ours. It's five hundred square miles."

"Five hundred?" Sally repeated, stupidly, just as Jo had done. "*Miles*?"

"Miles. I'm only just beginning to realise what we've let ourselves in for."

"But surely," Sally went on, "it's only to us it seems enormous. Ross Andrews has presumably been able to cope. Is there any reason why he shouldn't just because we're here?"

"None. Except he doesn't intend to stay," Jo replied flatly.

Sally stared at her sister. "You mean he's walking out, just because we've come?"

"Something like that. It's not so much his disapproval of us personally—although heaven knows he couldn't have expressed that much more strongly—but rather the fact that Nyala could become ours. He claims we're just a couple of novices and that Nyala should really go to the State. They would run it properly and presumably subsidise it."

Sally slumped in her chair. "I suppose if we were honest we'd admit that he was right."

"How do we know after one night here?" Jo cried passionately. "How do we know he hasn't just got us on a piece of string, that the Government isn't bribing him to get rid of us?"

"But . . . but it's unthinkable!"

"Is it? Sal, if you'd been yourself last night, if you'd sat with him for half the evening, been aware enough to see the way he looked at us, the way he spoke to us! After that nothing seems unthinkable. The point is, are we going to let him push us out?"

"Have we any alternative?" Sally countered.

Jo did not answer. She was a born fighter, but she suspected that this was one fight she might have to surrender before it had begun. There were quite a lot of jobs she would have tackled, even without experience, but she did not think that coping with wild animals was one of them. If Ross Andrews left there was the probability that the African rangers might go too. He would have won anyway then because they would be forced to go to the Government for help.

"We could advertise," Jo said hopefully.

"And get some other game reserve's throw-out? We wouldn't know any difference."

Jo stood up. "Well, I'm not beaten yet. Somehow, without having to crawl, we're going to make him see reason."

"But I'm not a reasonable man. Surely you've found that out already, Miss Fraser?"

34

Both girls swung round to the open door of the verandah. He had come up to them as silently as his lion and was leaning against the open door, his arms folded, a faintly amused smile on his face.

Jo flushed, but her voice was cold. "Listeners never hear good of themselves, Mr. Andrews."

"Touché." He turned to Sally. "I'm glad you're looking a little better this morning. Did you sleep well?"

"Marvellously, thank you."

"There's one thing about this area—the nights are often cool. In fact they can be extremely cold."

Sally looked from her sister to Ross Andrews. Jo made good friends quickly and easily, but she also made bad enemies. It was time to step in and act as peacemaker.

"Jo tells me you're not going to stay on at Nyala, Mr. Andrews."

"She's quite right."

"Then you must have made the decision before we came. It might have been kinder to stop us making such a long journey."

He shook his head. "My decision was taken last night only."

"Then you mean you made your judgement after meeting us at the end of that long journey. In fact you could hardly say you met me. So after only an hour or so you decided you couldn't work with my sister. It doesn't really seem fair."

He eyed her thoughtfully. "Probably you've had a one-sided version of what happened last night. I really think your sister believes I set a lion on her. Mind you, I suppose it's as good a way as any to get rid of visitors. I must bear it in mind next time."

Now he was laughing at her. Jo glared at him. She never had been very good at coping with people she did not understand. "So you really are leaving?"

"We can only run Nyala on my terms, Miss Fraser," he answered inexorably.

"And those are?"

"That you hand Nyala over to the State immediately."

Jo was about to leap in when Sally forestalled her with a touch on the arm.

"That's hardly fair, Mr. Andrews," she pointed out gently. "We don't even know yet what is potentially ours. We've seen nothing but this and our two rooms. You tell us there are difficulties, but we haven't the slightest idea what they are . . ."

Before he could answer Kari ran across the garden and up the steps and started to talk swiftly and with some agitation, pointing to somewhere in the distance beyond the house.

Andrews nodded. "All right, we'll leave in ten minutes. Have the truck ready and my guns." And as Kari disappeared he turned back to the girls. "I'm sorry, we'll have to continue this some other time. Poachers—by all accounts a fairly large gang. I shall be away most of the day, probably."

"Are you going in the truck?" Jo asked.

He nodded briefly.

"Then I'm coming. What do I need?"

For a second she thought he was going to argue, but he merely shrugged. "As you wish. As long as you know I'm telling you—in front of your sister—that we're not going for a picnic."

"I'm aware of that."

"Then put on some long cotton trousers and something with sleeves. You'll need a hat and a pair of comfortable shoes—not sandals. And some of that insect repellent I told you to buy. Oh, yes, and a heavy jersey in case we're back late." He paused, turning. "And you, Miss Sally Fraser?"

Sally smiled. "I would only be a nuisance. No, I'm going to potter about here for the day and find my bush feet, or whatever you call it."

"Fine. Saku will help you with anything you want. Oh, and Miss Fraser . . ."

"Sally," she corrected.

"Sally, then. If you do see a stray lion wearing a leather collar also pottering about the place, don't be alarmed, I really won't have sent her back to frighten you."

Sally laughed aloud. "I think you're human after all, Mr. Andrews!"

"Ross. But don't run either. Goldie will only think you're playing."

When the ten minutes were up, Jo was waiting in the shade of the Land-Rover. When Ross Andrews arrived he gave her a cursory inspection which she assumed to have passed because he made no comment except to nod her into the passenger seat. In the back were Kari and two young Africans.

"I like your sister," were the first words he spoke after they had driven away from the perimeter of the house along a narrow dusty track.

"Everybody likes Sally," Jo answered simply. "I don't know what my brother and I would have done without her."

"I was beginning to think you gave the orders."

"Only sometimes, and only because she lets me. But you always know when you've gone too far with Sally."

The track wound its way directly across the bush, through scrub and thorn trees and everywhere the white, blowing sand of the desert. Here and there were clumps of trees, wild fig mostly, he told her, and a few thorn bushes. A herd of impala came across the track, their graceful leaps bringing the truck to a halt. And before Ross Andrews started again he pointed to a clump of trees and an almost imperceptible movement.

"Zebra!" she exclaimed in delight. But today there was no time to stop and wonder at the game, the giraffe that munched away at leaves high above their heads, unconcerned at the humans passing so near. Buck there were in plenty, and a shy old kudu bull hiding behind some thorn trees.

The day had started well and Jo wanted it to remain one of truce. So she decided : no personal questions, no talk of wills or resignations. Instead she said, as they slowed down once more over a particularly bumpy part of the track, "Tell me about the poachers. What are they after? Ivory?"

"Some. Others just want free meat. I suppose any ranger would tell you there are four kinds of poachers. The first we see little of up here. He's the white man who merely wants to boast of a kill. He'll go out at night with a light or gun and shoot anything that moves— mostly harmless cattle. Fortunately there are few enough white men here and those that are know the rules of the game too well.

"The tribal poacher is after gain. He wants to sell his meat. He carries a gun which he doesn't always know how to use properly. It's usually through him that wounded—and dangerous—game are left to drag out their last days in the bush.

"Some poachers hunt in packs. They carry spears and usually have half-starved dogs with them. The dogs can follow the game until it gives up and then there's the spear for the last thrust. Today we are after the worst kind of poachers—those who use traps. They've probably come over the border from Rhodesia knowing we have fewer rangers out in the field. But all poachers are a pretty nasty breed. They kill for greed, not hunger. Only the Bushmen kill because they're hungry. And we tend to turn a blind eye to them as long as they only kill in the dry season."

"I heard that my uncle knew the Bushmen well."

"No one knows the Bushmen well. A few have chosen comparative civilisation, the villages near the rivers, particularly up by the swamp land, but the nomad tribes grow increasingly shy and stay in the desert, driving a few cattle, growing a few meagre crops. Your uncle used to spend a week, whenever he had the time, right out in the desert. He would take Kari with him and they would use every means to make contact with the Bushmen, even to photograph them." He looked up into the heavy hazy heat of the morning sky. "This will be a bad season for them. The drought has gone on too long already."

From the back Kari spoke excitedly and a few moments later Ross Andrews pulled off the main track, across the scrub. Here there was no shelter from the brassy glare of the sun and on the hard, uneven surface it seemed that the truck had lost all its springs. They halted finally in a clearing and without a glance towards her Ross Andrews climbed down, followed by the three Africans. After a second's hesitation Jo followed them. She could not keep back the gasp of horror.

The vicious teeth of a trap were still holding the broken end of a once slender foot. The buck, with sad, sad eyes, lay there whimpering in her last agony. Not only was the shattered leg a mass of sharp bone and blood, but one of the haunches had been ripped open. Jo turned quickly away. A second later she heard the crack of a rifle and when she looked again the eyes were glazed and at rest.

Ross Andrews face was hard and bleak. "There's your poacher for you. The touble is he doesn't even check his snares, so the animal is left to die of pain and thirst and at the mercy of other predators. You see," he pointed with his gun as a brown shape slunk round the bush and came out to watch them. "Hyena, bold as brass. He knows now he can have the rest of the kill." Abruptly he turned to Kari. "Well, have you found the tracks?"

"Towards the water hole, *Morena*."

"Well, we'll try, but I don't hold out much hope. You'd better wait in the truck, Miss Fraser, we'll be about half an hour."

"Can't I come?"

He hesitated only briefly. Already she had discovered he was a man who made his mind up instantly. "If you like. But this isn't the English countryside, you know, and the temperature is around a hundred."

She lifted her chin. "I'm aware of that. Would you prefer that I spent my three months in a deck chair in the garden?"

He started across the uneven ground, with one African behind him, then herself with Kari and the other taking up the rear, probably at a pace far slower than his usual one. She thought she would have been nervous, but oddly enough was not, although she remembered distinctly that in her book about the Kruger Park it was strictly forbidden ever to get out of a car.

In front of her Ross held up his hand and the small party was instantly still. Not more than fifty yards away a great herd of blue-black beasts, with tossing horns and shaggy heads, crossed their track as though on the march. There could have been a hundred of them, and Jo held her breath in wonder at being so close to her first real game.

When Ross turned back to her she raised her eyebrows in query and his answer came back as a whisper. "Wildebeest." Then the herd was suddenly alerted to their presence and, like a troop of drilled cavalry, they were thundering out of the bush in a tight, almost dancing formation.

They came to within a few yards of the water-hole and the air already smelled sweeter, fresher, and the camel-thorns no longer rasped at their clothes. Under a clump of trees at the far side two giraffe munched at the high leaves and a few zebra raced away into the distance.

Ross and Kari were on their knees examining the tracks, but it did not take them long to decide that it was not worth continuing. As she stood and watched them Jo became deeply aware of the sun. There was no shade, no escape from it, but she was determined he should not see her discomfort.

Back in the truck she thought Ross Andrews had given up the chase, but she discovered he was merely trying to outflank his enemy. Oh, yes, he told her, he knew in which direction the poachers had gone, on foot, about half a day ahead, probably heading for one of the villages on the edge of the great salt-pan. But with the drought setting in one of their number would be almost certain to check the snares.

Within fifteen minutes they found another victim—a buck too, but this time he was dead. Ross Andrews cursed aloud and then, at the same time as Jo, he became aware of the faint movement under the thick bush near the dead animal. Cautiously he moved aside the leaves and lifted up a baby fawn, thin and emaciated, probably near starvation. The brown, liquid eyes offered a silent plea for help.

Jo looked at Ross Andrews. "Will it live?"

"Not in the bush without its mother. It hasn't a hope; it can't be more than a few days old."

"Then what will you do?"

"Either finish it off here while we go on after the poachers, or take it back with us. Even then it has no more than a fifty-fifty chance."

She met his gaze steadily. "But that's what you're going to do, isn't it?"

"I imagine you're not offering me any choice. Come on, Kari, get going. You'd better drive while I try to get some water down it." He spoke as if he gave in grudgingly, so she was not sure whether his decision would have been different had she not been there.

Suddenly Jo shivered. "Is there always so much death in the bush?"

"Always. But there's life too. That's what the bush is

about, the simple matters of life and death. All animals have to kill to live. I told you before, Miss Fraser, it's a cruel country. I'm only here to preserve it from human destruction, to give all the game a better chance, away from the hunters' guns."

The tiny animal in his arms moved slightly and the eyes flickered as Ross Andrews put a rag soaked in water into its mouth. Twice it tried to suck the moisture, but the effort was too much as it slumped back again.

Jo touched the tiny, silky head. "It's dead too, isn't it?"

"Not yet. There's still a chance, only a small one."

"I want it to live," Jo said simply, "not just because it's young, and frightened and motherless, but because it seems like a symbol. My first day at Nyala."

". . . You mean a symbol of hope that you should keep Nyala."

"If you like—yes." She added curiously, "Where will you go, Mr. Andrews?"

"To another job like this. It's all I know, all I care about."

"Have you ever been to England?"

"Oh, yes, I lived there for several years. But I never want to go back permanently. It would squeeze me dry. Once you've known a place of immense freedom, where a man can still be alone and pit his wits against nature, you would never want to go back."

"You don't like humans very much, do you?"

There was the faintest ghost of a smile. "Let's just say I prefer the company of animals. They're more predictable."

They reached the bungalow in time for a late lunch, but Jo knew she would not be able to think of eating until she saw what chance the tiny fawn had. In a small thatched building near the house that seemed to be fitted up as a makeshift surgery Ross Andrews started to feed the animal drip by drip with warm milk from a baby's bottle.

For a while Jo watched, then she said quietly, "I think I could manage that if you have other things to do."

"Then hold her comfortably as you would a child; it will be a long job—she's only taking a few drops now and then."

Two hours later Jo was still there, absorbed in her self-appointed task. Ross had looked in on her once, but made no comment. She had volunteered to do this, so presumably she must be left to get on with it. Her arms ached from holding them in the same position, but suddenly the tiny body wriggled and then the eyes opened in fear. The fawn was coming to life.

She called and soon one of the servants brought Ross. He took the struggling animal from her and nodded, pleased with what he saw. "I reckon she'll make it after all. We'll put her in one of the cages and let her sleep."

Jo looked down at the tiny creature curled up on clean straw. "She really is straight out of Walt Disney, isn't she?" she said softly.

"Yes, but I warn you, if you keep her here, you'll find you have more than a puppy on your hands. She'll follow you wherever you go."

Laughter bubbled up in Jo. "I really won't mind that. She is my symbol after all, isn't she?"

He shook his head, smiling. "You're a strange one. One minute a fighting cat, the next . . ."

"Yes?"

"Never mind." His voice changed abruptly. "I should take a rest. You'll be useless to everyone dead on your feet." He turned on his heel and left the room.

In the sitting room Jo found Sally, who confessed she had been sleeping most of the day but really did feel herself again now. "And you, Jo. How did the trip go? I imagine you didn't catch the poachers?"

"No, but we destroyed two of their traps—vicious-looking steel things. If you'd seen, Sally, what they'd done to the animals!" She shuddered.

"You look just about all in. Don't forget, you may think you can ride roughshod over this climate, but I say treat it with respect, or it'll get you sooner or later. Did you talk to Ross Andrews about leaving?"

Jo shook her head. "No, there was no chance. Besides, if he wants to go how are we going to stop him? We're the last people he'll listen to. Why, he even admitted he preferred animals to people. Oh, he knows how to treat *them* all right."

"Then he won't walk out of Nyala, will he?" Sally said calmly.

"That's just what he *is* going to do, out of spite. He doesn't want us here and I daresay he doesn't much care how he gets us out."

Sally leaned forward. "Listen, you idiot, of course he wants to get us out, but from what you've said *he* doesn't want to leave." She looked swiftly round and lowered her voice. "You've only confirmed what I was thinking this afternoon. Nyala is his life. Do you honestly believe, if he has any feelings at all for the animals, he's going to walk out of here and leave them to be cared for by a couple of green girls? Of course not. He's counting on us believing his threat and going home at the end of the week. But if we stand our ground . . ."

Jo caught her breath. "You're right, I really believe you're right, Sal. But what are we going to say to him?"

"Nothing. Pretend he never said anything about leaving. And Jo . . ."

"Yes?"

"Curb your temper. I can see he's a difficult character, but don't bait him or tell him what you think of him."

"That will be difficult," Jo said bluntly. "I guess he's been too used to having his own way round here. And whatever he says I believe he thought Uncle Harold would leave this place to him."

Sally laid a hand on Jo's trouser-clad leg. "Maybe you're right, but don't be too sure. We've been here less than twenty-four hours. It's no time or place to make snap judgements."

When Jo reached her room she realised she was almost more tired than she had been yesterday. She had had several hours of the most intense heat of her life. She had tried to take in so many unfamiliar sights and sounds and she had just spent two hours almost immobile in a stifling little room with a sick animal. Derbyshire seemed a million miles away.

She flung herself down on top of the sheets, and slept and dreamed, and when she woke the room was dark and the air cool at last. At first she thought the thumping on her door was part of a dream, but then the catch snapped and framed in the light was Goldie, sitting on her haunches.

Even now there was a sudden spurt of fear, but she pushed it down quickly.

"Hello, Goldie." Her voice was almost steady.

The lioness padded to her bedside and watched, with that unnerving stare.

Now what? thought Jo. I haven't quite got the courage to get up while she's here, neither do I want to call out and make her think I'm alarmed. So she talked in normal tones, then reached out and tickled the alert ears. Her reward was a huge paw placed on the bed. She swallowed, hard.

"Who on earth are you chatting to? Oh . . ." Sally stood in the doorway uncertainly. "I've only seen her in the distance. Are you all right?"

"I think so. I'm just not quite sure whether I can calmly get up and walk out."

"I'll get Ross."

"*No*! I'm damned if I'll ask his help. Go on, Goldie, out, out!"

But the lioness took this to mean the exact opposite.

45

With one comfortable leap she was on the end of the bed, her great weight resting comfortably on Jo's bare toes.

"Oh, lord, now I can't even get up if I want to."

"Then I am going to fetch Ross. Pride can be carried too far, even in our family."

But Ross was already there. With his hands on his hips he looked in, his eyes glinting with amusement. "I'm afraid," he said gravely, "you look like having some fatal fascination for lions and fawns, just as beds have a fascination for Goldie. She simply can't resist one. If you move she won't take the slightest bit of notice of you. She'll simply think she's commandeered your bed for good."

"Then I'd better show her who's boss, hadn't I?" And acting more bravely than she felt she pushed, with feet and hands, until the great body flopped to the floor. Goldie gazed at her with an expression of great sorrow, but, with what dignity she could muster, walked out.

When Jo had showered and changed she heard laughter coming from the sitting room. Well, Sally wasn't wasting any time coming to terms with Mr. Ross Andrews. But she bore her sister no resentment because that was Sally's way. She never had liked to be at war. For just a moment Jo hesitated outside her own room. Perhaps she should stay out and let Sally do the negotiating . . .

Goldie rose in her corner to greet Jo, then thought better of it and slumped lazily back into sleep. But, as Ross Andrews stood up, so did an alert brown body. Not another lion, surely, was her first thought. Then she saw that it was a dog, mostly boxer.

"Sherry?" Ross Andrews said politely, "or would you like something longer?"

"Sherry will do fine now that it's cooler."

As he handed her the glass he said, "You'd better come and meet one of the other members of the family." He indicated the dog who had not moved a muscle since

46

she came into the room. "This is Tau—a foolish name really since in the local language it means lion. But we didn't have Goldie when Tau joined us. Even when he was a puppy the boys used to say he was as brave as a lion, so the name stuck." He nudged the dog with his shoe. "But he's not so much of a house pet as Goldie. He's trained purely as a hunting dog. Normally I never go into the bush without him, but we thought yesterday he had picked up some kind of bug."

"How about the fawn?" Jo asked eagerly. "Is she still all right?"

"So it seems. We're having an hourly watch on her. She's taken a little more milk and now is sleeping again."

Tonight, Jo decided, he appeared more relaxed. Sally's doing probably, but she felt no resentment towards the sister who had such a calming influence on her life. If Sally could somehow make Ross Andrews see reason then she, Jo, might avoid losing her temper, or much worse, having to grovel.

The two sisters could not have been more opposite either in temperament or in looks. Jo had always been the outgoing one, rushing headlong into life, meeting new people, new experiences, with the enthusiasm that had been inherited from her father. She had also inherited his fiery temper, his generosity and his absolute honesty. Much of her character showed in her face, green eyes flecked with gold that seemed to catch fire when she was really angry; the same reddish glints in her silky hair. Usually she wore it to her shoulders, but had had it cut to a more manageable length before leaving England. Now it hung straight and even round her almost heart-shaped face. Jo had always been the first of the family to laugh, the one who loved to play a practical joke. People either admired Jo, or else they thought her too outspoken. They never guessed how uncertain she was underneath, how deeply she needed someone of her own to love.

47

She had been quite right when she said that everyone loved Sally. All the right fairy godmothers had been around when her sister was christened, endowing her with beauty, brains and a true gentleness of spirit. It still remained a mystery to Jo why Sally had not married. But if her sister was warm and gentle, she could also be very stubborn.

Her looks came just as directly from her mother who had been dark with intensely blue eyes. Sally also had her slender build with small hands and feet and an air—not completely true—of great delicacy. Jo used to say that beside her sister she sometimes felt like a clumsy giant. She never realised that her tall proud carriage drew many admiring glances.

Jo was day-dreaming. She came to hearing Sally and Ross talking about the problems of Nyala.

"What do you think," Sally was asking, "Uncle Harold would have done had he lived another few years? Did he talk about the future of Nyala?"

"Yes, sometimes. I think he honestly believed he could keep this place on its feet. Because he didn't talk much about his private affairs I assumed he was hoping to put in more capital. I didn't know things had gone as far as they had."

"As far as what?" Jo challenged.

He shrugged. "Well, for example, we need a new truck badly and there simply is not the money to buy one. Fortunately I cover a fair part of the reserve on horseback."

Sally looked at him wonderingly, forgetting the immediate question of finance. "But isn't that dangerous?"

"I often have the feeling that Nyala is much less dangerous than Piccadilly Circus. Every car and bus is a lethal weapon, so you regard them with caution. The same with animals. They only attack when provoked, wounded or very hungry; you learn to treat them with healthy respect. The exception to the rule is the rhino. It will charge without any reason at all. It rather likes to pretend it's an immovable object and wait in ambush for the unwary passer-by. There's only one escape if you're on foot, and that's to go for the nearest tree. Even then it's a question of whose patience holds out longest."

"Why?" said Sally curiously.

"An awkward rhino has been known to keep his hostage up that tree for several hours. But if you think I'm trying to frighten you," and here he was looking at Jo, "then I must tell you that there are no rhinos in Nyala."

But while Jo was just as interested in the wildlife of Nyala, she was determined not to be sidetracked from the more important issues of money. Three months suddenly seemed a very short time.

"Mr. Andrews. . . ." she started.

"Ross. Even if we're to be at war it's still simpler."

"Ross, then." Jo shrugged. "I was wondering what you and my uncle did to try to make Nyala pay its way."

"Like what?"

"Like getting the tourists in. Taking them out on safari . . ."

"You've been seeing too many Hollywood films."

She flushed. What did he think she was—a child?

"Perhaps you haven't seen enough," she threw back, "or rather you haven't learned the lessons of other parks. The Kruger, for instance. They encourage tourists from all over the world. I imagine they couldn't make the place pay without tourists."

He sighed. "We couldn't do it here,"

"Why not?"

"Because we haven't the facilities."

Jo was beginning to wonder if she would ever get the better of this man. "I don't understand you," she said at last. "You want Nyala to go to the State, yet surely that's the first thing they would do—encourage visitors." She appealed to her sister. "Don't you think so, Sal?"

"Yes . . . yes, I think you're right." In a quiet, but very determined way she said to Ross, "You could help us if you wanted to, Ross. You must realise that without you there would be no Nyala."

"There are other game rangers."

But Sally went on inexorably: "Did you get on with Uncle Harold? Was he a man to admire?"

"I never met a finer man in my life," was his answer.

Now it was Jo's turn. "Then you can't let him down, can you?"

He stood up and for just a second looked from one sister to another. The expression in his eyes was unreadable, even a little frightening. Then, without another word, he turned and strode out of the room.

CHAPTER FOUR

IT was nearly twenty-four hours before they saw Ross again. When questioned, Saku said that *Morena* was out working.

"Sulking, you mean," Jo muttered.

But after breakfast they were brought a note that he had left. It said briefly that he and Kari were out on trek today on horseback. It would be too tough to consider taking them. But tomorrow he had to go farther afield by truck to inspect some water-holes and he would be glad to give them at least a partial tour of the property. For today would they please stay within the perimeter of the house and adjoining land. They would be perfectly safe as long as they did not do anything foolish.

"Well," snorted Jo, "his opinion of us grows higher by the hour. What does he think we are—a couple of complete dimwits?"

"I think," said Sally more charitably, "he doesn't understand much about women. He honestly doesn't quite know what to make of us. We're more or less dumped on his doorstep as the possible new owners of the place that's been his home for four years. I think his reaction is probably quite natural."

"I really believe you're on his side," cried Jo.

"Not necessarily. I'm merely trying to see his point of view. If his only thought is for the preservation of the game, then we must seem like intruders . . ."

"If," said Jo darkly.

"Oh, Jo, don't think the worst of him just yet. I know he hasn't much in the way of social manners, but does that honestly matter? I can think of plenty of people I've worked with quite amicably, while I don't think much of them personally. After all, it isn't as though we've come out here as brides for Mr. Ross Andrews."

Jo raised her eyes in mock despair. "Heaven preserve us!"

"Well, then . . ."

Jo suddenly grinned. "You may be right, I don't know, but at least I'll try to reserve judgement for a week. I just have the feeling he's going to rub me up the wrong way, although he rather likes you. I think what worries me most is the fact that we have to take his word on everything. Any decision he makes about which we're doubtful there simply isn't anyone else to turn to—a neighbour, another man who knows the country."

"There's Neil Brand," Sally said tentatively.

"Sixty miles away, and anyway if he was a pal of Uncle Harold's then he's almost certain to be hand in glove with Ross Andrews. I'd like someone around like Bruce."

"Bruce Farley?" Sally's eyes widened. "Now you're confusing infatuation with common sense!"

For the first time since their arrival Jo felt a spurt of anger towards her sister. "Just because you didn't approve of him," she challenged. "You were all wrong about Bruce—simply because he didn't fit into yours and Alan's idea of the kind of man I should marry."

"He was a wanderer."

"Even wanderers settle down," Jo retorted. "Besides, I wasn't really thinking of my own feeling for him. I was thinking that he'd spent years in Africa. He knows something about it which we don't."

"Africa is a big continent," Sally reminded her. "It's possible that a reserve up here has entirely different problems from one, say, in Kenya. Anyway, Bruce— but it won't help much. Let's get down and do something practical today. Let's explore as far as we can and by the time we see Ross again at least we could make some suggestions instead of sitting back and grumbling."

Of course Sally was right. She generally was when it came to finding a way out of difficulties.

Before the full heat of the day was on them they set off to explore the immediate land round the house. From under her place in the shade Goldie rose, made a beeline for Jo, then waited expectantly.

Sally said, "Ross was right when he said you'd made a hit with her. I imagine she's going to come with us whether we invite her or not. Do you mind?"

Jo's attachment to Goldie was also beginning to grow. "No, in fact I think I'd be rather glad to have her protection. Who knows what we might meet?" In an excess of bravery she slapped Goldie's rump. "Although I'm not sure that *you* would be any more use than a cocker spaniel in an emergency!"

They started round the back of the house where most of the outbuildings were. Their first call was to the 'surgery' where the fawn's cage had been brought out to the shade and she lay stretched out. Already she was much stronger, for as they approached, she tried to struggle to her feet. Jo reached through the bars and touched her silky coat. "Hello there," she whispered, "you're going to be all right, aren't you?" The tiny animal did not flinch from her touch, but rather seemed to nuzzle at her finger.

Jo laughed aloud in delight. "What are we going to call her, Sal?"

"I don't know," Sally said, "you must name her. She's going to be yours. It's strange, you really do have a way with animals. I never knew it."

"Nor did I," Jo replied. "There's never been really time at home even to have a dog or cat. And yet I do remember when I was about ten or eleven collecting everything from the woods I could lay my hands on."

Sally pulled a face. "Toads included; mice and voles and that poor old duck with a limp—Jemima Puddle-duck." Both girls giggled.

Jo said suddenly, "I remember reading in a book that the name Holly meant good luck. Well, I think she's going to bring both of us luck. We'll call her Holly. Look, even Goldie seems to accept her."

Goldie was stretched out in the sun watching them all lazily, but making no attempt to disturb the fawn.

"One day," Jo said slowly, "I suppose Goldie will learn to kill helpless animals like that. It seems too awful to think of."

"Then don't get too starry-eyed about Nyala," Sally said practically, "I imagine we might see some pretty horrifying things before we leave here. Lions have to eat, the same as buck do."

"I suppose so, but I don't want to think about it. Come on or it will soon be too hot to walk."

Beyond the 'surgery' was the big open-sided cook-house, with an iron range just outside. Sally regarded it professionally. "I believe that could feed a dozen people or more—like a huge barbecue."

"And over there," Jo pointed. "They look like the perfect guest huts. I've seen pictures of them in some of the books I've been reading. They're called ron-davels."

"My, you have been doing your homework! But you're quite right." The three huts stood away from the house on a patch of scrubby grass. They were round, whitewashed, with a thatched roof rising to a point and a couple of windows each. Inside each was a wooden-framed bed and a couple of plain wooden chairs.

"That's exactly what they are," Sally commented, "sort of guest cottages. With a little paint and some freshening up they could be perfect. I wonder why

Ross said there were no facilities. These must have been used in the past. Well, I suppose he has his reasons."

As they walked farther, they kept on talking, trying to work out some plan of campaign. In a way the whole project fell neatly into two. If Jo could concentrate on learning as much about the actual running of the reserve as possible, since that seemed her natural bent, then Sally would put all her energies to the domestic side. They were both agreed that the only obvious way to make Nyala pay was through visitors.

"This afternoon," Sally said, "as soon as I've had a thorough look round I'm going to shut myself away and work out some facts and figures. I'll see what real possibilities the kitchen has and where Saku gets his supplies. The trouble is that by the look of things Ross and Uncle Harold have always lived on local produce. heaven knows what that meat we ate last night was— not any of the things we are used to eating, that's certain. What we would need is a deep-freeze. We've got our own generator, so electricity won't be any problem . . ."

"I think," Jo interrupted, "there are two things you're overlooking."

"What are they?"

"One—money."

"And?"

"Ross Andrews."

"You mean in case he objected?" Sally frowned.

"Not exactly. Look, let's walk on to the river and I'll tell you when I've got my thoughts sorted out. At least there's some shade over there."

They circled the house and walked down the sloping ground to the edge of the river. It wasn't very much as rivers go and the water was low.

At the point where it touched Nyala's 'garden' it was probably no more than thirty feet wide, but surprisingly clear, undoubtedly, Sally pointed out, from the lightness of the desert sand. As they bent to gaze into the glassy calm, a silver shoal of tiny fish raced through the shallows where a mass of feathery papyrus threw a ten-foot shadow across the water. But most beautiful of all were the waterlilies, their white, waxy flowers glistening in the sun. For a moment it seemed as if they were looking down into an English ornamental pool on a hot Sunday afternoon. Small, sharply black and white birds swooped along the bank, in and out of the colonies of nests that seemed to be suspended from the reeds. Then there were others with long red tail feathers and a glossy blue-crested head; tiny birds that darted from one tree to another in search of insects.

"It's like paradise!" Sally breathed.

Even as she spoke there was a movement among the thicker reeds a little farther downstream. Instinctively both girls walked towards it.

"I thought it was a big fish," Jo said, disappointed. "No, it's a floating log."

But the log kept moving until it came to the shallows, then the great appalling square-jawed mouth rose slowly from the water and they were both momentarily hypnotised by the stare of the bulging, ruby-red eyes. Beside them Goldie gave a deep, menacing growl and the spell was broken.

Sally tugged at Jo's hand and pulled her back from the river's edge so sharply that she nearly fell. When they turned back again the great ridged back of the crocodile was again underwater and the river, except for a narrowing circle of ripples, was calm again.

"Paradise!" echoed Jo, horrified.

Sally recovering from the shock, smiled slightly. "Well, even in the real paradise there was a serpent. And apparently even Goldie disapproves of crocodiles."

But Jo would not be drawn back to the river and

56

moved instead to the shade of a cluster of wild fig trees where she could watch the colourful bird life, darting, flashing colours from a dozen jewels, and forget the menace that lurked beneath the waters.

"I think," she said, "I'm going to feel about crocodiles as you do about snakes."

"Perhaps," Sally said sombrely, "but at least you know a crocodile sticks to the river. I imagine you could trip over a snake anywhere. Anyway," she changed the subject quickly, "you were going to tell me your ideas on safari guests at Nyala."

"Yes." Jo sat down on the hard ground, cupping her chin in her hand, frowning in her effort to sort out her thoughts.

"Well, it's like this," she began at last. "I too think the only way to make this place pay is to have visitors. I'm not worried about the domestic and catering arrangements. We can get round that somehow. But we're not going to persuade people to come to Nyala unless they can go out into the bush and view the game at first hand."

"Yes, that's right."

"Well, I presume most of them will be as green as we are. They can't go unaccompanied, so who on earth is going to act as guide? I can't honestly see Ross Andrews devoting his days to potted tours with unwelcome tourists, can you, Sal?"

"Oh, lord, I hadn't thought of that." Then, more hopefully, "But you can drive through the Kruger and other parks in your own car. What's different about Nyala?"

"The roads, I imagine, or the lack of them. You'd have to have a Land Rover or something similar. The springs of an ordinary car simply wouldn't last on even the short journey I did yesterday."

"Perhaps," said Sally in a small voice, "that's what he meant by lack of facilities."

"Perhaps." Jo's green eyes flashed. "But we're not going to give up as easily as that. What do you think the main things we need are—apart from a guide?"

"Money," said Sally bluntly, "the more you look at it, the more obvious that becomes. To get even one small party here we need a new truck, a deep-freeze and a few more home comforts. That's just basic. And from what Ross said, there isn't even enough money to replace the present truck."

"It's all what Ross says, isn't it? How do we know he's speaking the truth?"

"We don't, but I think he is—at least as far as the position at Nyala is concerned. Anyway, I daresay we can find out from Mr. Scott the exact amount of money available."

The more they talked the more it became apparent that every turning they took led to Ross Andrews. They could take no decisions without him.

By now the heat beating down upon them was immense. Even Goldie had abandoned them to stretch out and doze. So they made their way back to the house for cold drinks that Saku always seemed to have waiting for them.

Sally started to question him about the kitchen. Yes, he had once cooked for many people on the big range, but mostly he used the smaller one inside. Yes, there was a refrigerator—which he called a cold box, but he did not know what a deep-freeze was.

"Where do you get your meat from?" Sally asked curiously.

He looked at her in the faintest of surprise. "Why, *Morena* shoots it. And the fish come from the river, of course. Where else, lady?"

"Of course," said Sally weakly. "Where else indeed?" When he had gone she turned to Jo. "We have a lot to learn about life in the raw, it seems. Do you think safari visitors would want to know what they were eating?"

"Sitting round the table here I think they would, but not if they really went out on safari, camping, etc. I imagine it's only the rich Americans who expect a refrigerated truck along with them."

After lunch Saku, obviously bidden by his master, suggested that the ladies should rest in the hottest part of the day. Sally agreed and went to lie down, but Jo was far too restless, her brain turning over and over all the insurmountable problems.

She looked out across the garden, into the bush, where the heat of the sun seemed to melt into the hazy distance. She suddenly had a great longing to cross the whole of the park and see the desert for herself. There was a great deal here she had to come to terms with, much to learn and a whole new life and climate to which to grow accustomed. But she had the awesome feeling that she would not mind not returning to England for a long, long time. And on the other side of the coin three months seemed an impossibly short time to achieve anything at all. On top of all that she wanted to learn and had the wrong teacher. She and Ross Andrews could know each other a lifetime and still be crossing swords.

Not wanting to go into the house yet, she wandered over to see Holly. The little fawn was awake and much stronger and when Jo put her hand into the cage was even able to stand upright with a little help. Very carefully Jo opened the cage door and lifted Holly out. The warm brown eyes regarded her with complete trust. There was not a single movement of fear. Under the silky brown coat the flesh was beginning to fill out. Any day now, except for feeding, Holly would be able to fend for herself. But would she be safe even in the garden? Jo wondered, remembering the crocodile within a stone's throw of the house. What animals prowled at night when the air was dark and still?

Ross Andrews came home in the late afternoon to find her asleep in the basket chair under the trees with Holly curled up in her arms like a kitten.

She woke to see him standing over her. For just a few seconds she could not think where she was and she looked at him as a stranger as he stood holding the bridle of his horse whose coat was black and shining with sweat. Then one of the servants came and led the tired animal away. Ross himself looked tired, his thin face drawn and rough with a day-old beard, his shirt clinging to his body.

She focused suddenly. "You look as if you've had a bad day."

"Rough enough, but I don't like the look of things out there. Two of the water-holes are far too low for comfort. I'm wondering what I shall find nearer the desert. The Bushmen say it's a year of bad omens."

"And do you believe in bad omens?"

He shrugged. "I believe in facts. In these parts omens and facts get confused. You have to learn to listen to the country speaking to you. It can tell you many things. And you have to listen to the natives. What they tell you usually has a grain of truth. Saku will tell you for instance that when the crocs move into the home stretch of the river it's going to be a bad season."

"There was a crocodile over there today," she said quietly.

"Where?"

She stood up and crossed the garden down to the banks of the river. She pointed down towards the white cluster of lilies just beginning to close. "It came from the opposite bank," she said, "and seemed to stare at us with red eyes. I had no idea that a crocodile could be so truly ugly. I'm afraid we didn't wait to see any more."

"They're nasty brutes all right, but you can make a

fascinating study of them. You remember asking about Neil Brand—well, he spends most of his leave crocodile-hunting up in the Okavango swamps. He'll talk to you for hours about their habits. By the way, I talked to him on the radio telephone early this morning and told him you and your sister had arrived, but he already knew by the bush telegraph. He's driving over here at the weekend with his son Sandy to welcome you—bringing a friend too, he said." He nodded towards the river. "We'll get him to make a couple of good handbags out of that fellow ... don't look so worried, I doubt if there are more than a couple of them about." He paused. "Did you and your sister have a good day?"

She nodded. "We tried to make a few plans. Sally says we can't carry any of them out without your help."

That cold, bleak look was back in his eyes. "I'd like to help, but I won't be here, will I?" He leaned back against the gnarled trunk of a tree and dug into his pocket for a pipe. He seemed a long time in lighting it. Finally he drew on it slowly and said, "Look, I have no objection to you two personally, whatever you may think. Why not let's call a truce and I'll give you a month's holiday to remember? Perhaps holiday is too strong a word. because we're short on time here, but I'll show you what life on a game reserve is really like."

Jo could feel her temper beginning to rise already, but she controlled it. Sally would have approved. "I too would like to call a truce ... Ross, but not for the ends you want. We haven't come here for a holiday, but to learn. Unfortunately we have to rely on an unwilling teacher. At least you might listen to our plans tonight without walking out on us."

He regarded her thoughtfully. "You're a very determined young woman, aren't you?"

She returned that gaze steadily. "I'm determined to see justice. Is that so great a crime? And it's not just for myself. I don't suppose you know anything about our family, do you?" And when he did not answer she went on: "My parents died five years ago leaving practically nothing. I was still at school, Sally was at college and our brother Alan was just beginning to get a foot in the hotel business. Alan worked day and night to help Sally and both of them took extra jobs to keep me at school. For five years it's been very tough indeed. Then suddenly the chance of a lifetime is dropped into our laps. An unknown uncle throws out a challenge to make up for those years. We accepted that from the beginning we hadn't got much chance of success, but we never guessed that the one person we counted on to give us a chance would set his face against us so strongly. That's what I mean by justice!"

For a long time he did not answer and she had no idea what effect her words had had on him. She only knew that it was the last time she intended to either bargain or appeal to him. There was simply nothing more she could say that would get through to him. She was not, as she said so strongly to Sally, going to grovel.

Suddenly he turned and smiled. For just a second she thought he was laughing at her again. This time she knew she would not be able to control that temper. But he held out his hand and she found herself taking it.

"Well, Miss Jo Fraser, I think I must declare you the winner."

"What ... what do you mean?"

"What do I mean? That will have to wait, until I've washed some of the filth of the bush from myself. Take Holly back to her cage, then go and get your sister. I'll meet you in the sitting room in fifteen minutes."

"But what ..."

"*But nothing*. Fifteen minutes."

She had not the slightest idea of his intentions, but she found herself meekly obeying him, first taking Holly back, having a quick wash herself and then rousing Sally.

"We've been called to a council meeting," she said solemnly, "but whether it's for war or peace we won't know for ten minutes."

"You're talking in riddles," Sally protested.

"Just like Ross Andrews. He's made some kind of final decision about us and the future of Nyala; but what it is I can only guess."

The dark tropical night had fallen with its imperceptible swiftness by the time he joined them with Tau at his side. First he called for Saku, who immediately appeared with drinks, then he relit his pipe.

Jo was watching him carefully. He had showered away the dirt, but some of the tiredness remained. He must, she decided, drive himself very hard indeed. There was not an ounce of spare flesh on his bones; he was a man not used to asking, or giving, quarter.

He looked only towards Sally. "I wish you'd heard the short lecture your sister gave me. She made me feel—and sound—the very worst sort of heel. I've thought hard about what she said, about what you both have said since you came, and I've decided she's right in one respect—that I haven't given you a fair chance. I haven't changed my views on what should eventually happen to Nyala, but I'm willing to try it your way for a couple of months. I think I can make you see I'm right, but in any case I can't stand by and watch Nyala run itself into the ground, so the better success we make now the better things will be in the future. But I must say," he warned, "that unless you two have a few spare thousand tucked away your chances are very small indeed."

Sally was still cautious. "You do really mean what you say, Ross? We will all be fighting on the same front?"

He nodded and suddenly he seemed less tired. "I mean it. I've probably become what you think I am—an uncivilised brute, like the croc out there." He reached for his glass and raised it. "From now on it's nothing but Nyala."

"Nyala," they both echoed, and Jo felt a sudden soaring sense of happiness. Perhaps Holly had been a symbol after all. But that would remain her private thought.

"There is just one thing," he said, "one condition to all this."

Jo looked at him sharply. He couldn't go back now, not after all that.

"I gather you both have made plans. Well, I'm willing to listen to them. I'm aware this portion of Nyala has many drawbacks. But as far as the actual game and the reserve is concerned, I expect to be obeyed instantly. Out there there are no second chances. You must abide by my decisions, which won't, I assure you, be taken lightly. And I warn you now too, I can be tough and bad-tempered, impossible to live with, but as long as you realise that everything I do is for Nyala, then we should be able to rub along."

He smiled the quick, sudden smile that Jo had glimpsed outside. "I think that must be the longest speech I've ever made in my life! It's about time I asked if you two have anything to say."

"Nothing," said Sally quietly, "except 'thank you'. I think we both realise it hasn't been easy for you. We'll just do what we can to help. In the long run it's all for Nyala, and at least we will have broadened our education."

"Right," he said briskly, "then let's get down to a few practical details."

So all that evening, with just a break for a meal when they still went on talking, they tried to work out a plan of campaign. Again and again they returned to the same old problems, lack of men and money.

Ross explained that he only had a staff of sixteen African game guards to help him, apart from Kari. And when Sally said that did not mean very much to her in terms of acres or square miles he told her that in the Kruger Park a ranger was generally in charge of a section of about eighty square miles—about five hundred thousand acres—and he had about twenty men to help him.

"I'm not saying we need that many here," he added quickly. "The Kruger Park is a highly organised place which is as much a tourist attraction as anything in Africa. I imagine they must have a million or more visitors in the course of a year. But we are understaffed here, especially in experienced men. When your uncle was alive one of us used to stay here while the other would go off on trek for two or three weeks at a time. Like that we managed to keep Nyala pretty well covered. Apart from anything else I'm worried about the poaching; the pressure is really on us and I can't always tell if the men at the outposts are completely reliable. I simply cannot get round and see them often enough."

"I suppose," said Sally, "you need another white ranger up here."

"I also need another truck," he told her, "and even more important I need to spend some money on pumping equipment at some of the water-holes. Water, or the lack of it, could be our downfall quicker than anything else."

Some of Jo's high spirits began to evaporate. "What you're saying is that if we're going to try to do any of the things that will put Nyala on the map, then we must have some money first."

He nodded. "That's just about it. I suppose that's what I was trying to tell you yesterday when you put up the idea of safaris. It is a good idea, but we can't do it on a large enough scale."

"But we could take about six people," Sally argued, "if we sold it to them the right way. Expensive, exclusive, but with the only home comforts actually at the bungalow. Five hundred miles of game to themselves. I think I could manage my end of the operation if I could get hold of a deep-freeze. People will take an awful lot of roughing it as long as they can rely on coming back to a shower and some good food."

He was suddenly thoughtful, his teeth clenched on his pipe. "One thing has just occurred to me. Neil Brand has a brother who runs a tourist agency in Jo'burg. I think he has a branch somewhere in the Republic. I have a feeling a fair amount of his business is sending people up to Chobe and the other national reserves. We could ask Neil on Sunday what he thinks the chances are of success here." He turned to Sally. "And I reckon we should order your deep-freeze anyway. There's enough money in the kitty to cover that. Besides, whatever happens at the end of the three months we'll be able to sell it. If you tell me what you want I'll put in an order on the radio telephone."

So it seemed a lot depended on Neil Brand. Jo remembered him as a friendly, easy-going man, although her mind's picture of him had become blurred over the year. Now was probably as good a time as any to ask Ross a question that had been mildly worrying her since their arrival.

"Ross. . ."

"You've got a solution to all our problems." He raised his eyebrows.

"No, I'm afraid not." Was he patronising her again? "It was you mentioning Neil Brand that put an idea into my head. You said you knew him quite well, and you heard about our existence about a year ago—after he returned from England, I assume. Have you any idea at all why I was never mentioned, not in the will so much, but even as a person? He must surely have told Uncle Harold there were three of us."

"I can't answer that. I only know that your uncle spoke of a nephew and niece in England. You'll have to ask Neil himself."

Jo turned to Sally. "You'll ask him, won't you, Sal? It will sound better from you. I suppose it's not important, but I'm terribly curious."

Sally suddenly stretched and yawned. "I don't think I can take any more discussion about anything," she said. "My brain's spinning as it is. And, Ross, what time did you say you wanted us up?"

"We ought to leave here at five-thirty. I'll get Saku to bring breakfast at five. That will give you half an hour to wake up."

Sally groaned, "I never was any good at getting up," but when Ross glanced at her she added quickly, "Don't worry, I shan't get ill or do anything stupid, it's just part of my temperament. Besides, soon I shall be too busy here to be taking trips out into the bush. That's going to be strictly Jo's line."

Ross was as good as his word. He was already waiting the following morning as the two sisters stumbled out, half asleep.

But once away from the house the air woke them up. It was crystal clear, sweet and cool, and truly the best time of day. In the east they could see the first fiery glow of the sun as it rose above the distant horizon of the bush. There was even a silvery pattern of dew on the grass. Impossible to believe that in two hours' time that same sun could become an instrument of torture.

"This is Nyala, at its best," Ross told them, "this is the time to see the best of the game. This is the time to bring the safari out and show them the perfection of Nyala. Between now and about seven-thirty you'll see more game than throughout the rest of the day. I wish I had time to stop and show you every animal. But not today. Today . . ." he stopped abruptly and spoke a few crisp words to Kari. Within seconds he had stopped the truck, then backed it into a screen of thorn trees just off the track.

"What . . ." Jo began.

"Don't ask questions, just wait."

For a few moments Jo was puzzled. The ground seemed to be shaking under them, as though racked by a series of small explosions. And then, on the very place where the truck had halted seconds before, came the leader of a magnificent herd of elephant.

They marched in stately splendour towards the river, from the huge-tusked bulls, smaller cows and a few calves being continually nudged into line by their parents. There must have been twenty or thirty of them, and Jo watched, spellbound, thinking it was worth coming all the way to Africa for just this moment. As the last one passed them it raised its trunk and the trumpeting must have been heard back at the house. It was like a great shout of triumph.

Ross waited a few moments before driving off. "You were lucky," he commented. "We don't have too big a herd in Nyala. Sometimes I've spent a week on trek and never caught sight of one. They must be short of water. They drink about fifteen gallons a day."

During the first part of that morning Ross pointed out a dozen different varieties of game, giraffe and zebra in plenty, springbok and the huge antelope called eland, several kudu bulls, buffalo and wildebeest and always the graceful springing herds of impala. They saw, briefly, their first wild lion and a pack of wild dogs. The latter, Ross told them briefly, was the only animal of the bush he really hated. Their cruelty was human cruelty, hunting in packs until their prey falters, exhausted, then ripping out pieces of living flesh.

Jo stored away all that day's knowledge, determined to learn as fast as she could and play an active part in the development of Nyala. Sally had her place clearly defined. It was up to her, Jo, to make Ross see that while she might be inexperienced in the bush, she was not afraid.

It was a long day and towards the end they were all tired. Although Sally did not complain, Jo knew she could not take this too often. The combination of heat and rough travel seemed to affect her badly.

They saw a fair amount of Nyala, as far as the scrubby bush broke into desert. Here for mile after mile there was not a single tree, not a patch of shade to escape the soaring temperature.

It was the water-holes that worried Ross. One had dried up completely, another was down to muddy silt. It was a poor lookout for the game.

They returned at dusk. The two girls were too tired to do more than wash and eat and tumble into bed. But Ross did offer a rare word of praise.

He had not known many people right out from England take to the bush as they had done. "I would like to let you down lightly," he said, "but there simply isn't the time."

The next day Jo stayed at home and helped Sally with the replanning of the house. Sally was also making many sorties into the kitchen and eventually confessed to Jo that she was supervising the Sunday meal herself. Although supplies were limited she wanted to show Ross just what kind of a spread could be put on for visitors.

"And this one just happens to be Neil Brand," Jo said slyly.

Sally flushed. "If you make more hints like that I'll

thump you! He just happens to be the visitor for tomorrow, and that's all. You're building something up that simply wasn't there. We met him in England for one day, that's all. Not much romance in that!"

"All right, I give in. I really was only teasing."

Ross was working in the early part of Sunday morning, but he was back at the house to receive their visitors. "I wonder," he said, as they watched the dust of the approaching truck, "who his visitor is. It will seem quite strange to see three fresh faces within a week."

A few minutes later the truck pulled up in the small circle outside the bungalow. Neil Brand stepped out and Jo's memory was instantly cleared. He came towards her and Sally with a smile. But suddenly her eyes were not on him, but on the man who got out from the passenger seat. She drew in her breath sharply. It couldn't be; it couldn't possibly!

"Hello there, Jo, welcome to Africa," called Bruce Farley.

CHAPTER FIVE

HE was even taller and bigger than she remembered. And with his skin bronzed by the sun and hair bleached to the colour of flax he was even more exciting than the man who had stormed in and out of her life a year ago. Bruce Farley had been the only man ever to make her feel dainty and completely feminine.

Now, as he strode towards her, his delight obviously matching her own, she felt ridiculously tongue-tied. He gripped both her shoulders and kissed her soundly on both cheeks.

"God, Jo, it's a miracle! I never expected to see you at the back of beyond like this." Then his hand was outstretched behind her, although she noticed with secret pleasure that his eyes flicked back to hers. "And Sally. Don't say the Frasers are here in force?"

Sally shook her head. "Not Alan, just us."

There were more greetings from Neil and then the two girls were shaking hands with the small, rather solemn boy who stood beside him, an almost exact replica of his father. He was trying to be polite and patient, but his bright blue eyes were darting all round.

It was Ross who came to his rescue, ruffling his hair and saying cheerfully, "Well, young Sandy, I know who you are waiting for. She's around somewhere. *Goldie*!" he roared.

With a great shout of delight Sandy flung himself at the lion who had appeared round the side of the house, burying his head in her neck as she nudged his back with her head. The only thing his father said, quite casually, was: "Remember what I told you about not running, Sandy. She's too heavy for you if she jumps."

71

Sally watched open-mouthed, then turned to Neil. "But there isn't an ounce of fear in him. Aren't *you* at all afraid?"

"No, only that Goldie doesn't know her own strength. They've been friends ever since Goldie came first as a cub. Sandy's pretty good with animals. He probably wouldn't be afraid if he stood in front of a rogue elephant. But Ross has taught him a hell of a lot of sense. I don't think he would do anything foolhardy."

As Ross led the way inside Jo and Bruce were separated. But she was intensely aware of him, impatient for the moment when they could be alone together. Then their eyes met and held, as if they were already touching each other.

"Beer, Farley?" That was Ross, sounding more cool and clipped than usual. For some reason she glanced across at him and surprised a look she did not recognise. Was it anger, distaste—Did he *really* think she was straight out of the schoolroom?

"Thanks," Bruce replied lazily. "While you're pouring it out I'll get Jo to show me the garden." he turned his very special smile on her.

"Of course." She was at his side immediately, and she did not attempt to move away when she felt his arm across her shoulders. Rather, she moved towards him. Let Mr. Ross Disapproving Andrews put that in his pipe and smoke it!

She led the way down to the river, but strangely, once they were alone she felt all her old uncertainty return. Was it a coincidence he was here, or . . .

"How did you know I . . . we were here?" she asked breathlessly.

He held her away from him, teasing, "Bush telegraph."

She sat down on the old tree stump in the shade of the fig trees. That way her legs felt steadier. Perhaps she was wrong after all. Perhaps her delight at seeing him was stronger than his after all. He hadn't even tried to kiss her.

"No, tell me, please. Nyala is a long way from anywhere, even by African standards."

"Perhaps, but not by diamond prospecting standards."

"You mean . . . you heard there were diamonds in this area." Her heart seemed to be squeezed inside her body. So it was diamonds that brought him here, not . . . She could hardly bear it.

"In a way." His eyes were bright as he went on : "It started when I was introduced to Neil in a pub just before I finally left Derbyshire—the day before, in fact. Someone thought we would have something in common, both working in Africa. He gave me his card and told me to give him a call if ever I came to this area. That's it really, except I got a tip about an old river bed that could possibly hold diamonds, so I wrote to him. He wrote back and invited me down for a few days, adding how extraordinary that a couple of people from the very town we met in were coming to Nyala. I merely told him to keep it a surprise from you."

Suddenly his voice thickened and the brightness in his eyes was piercingly strong. Then he held out his arms to her. "Come here, Jo, I can't stand it much longer." And then she was home at last with his mouth hard on hers, her body crushed to his. So it was going to be all right after all!

When finally, trembling, they drew apart he said, "It's been a long year, Jo. I behaved like a heel, didn't I?"

"There wasn't really anything between us," she lied. "I just wondered what had happened to you."

"Oh, well, I told you then I was a rotten letter writer. And I always intended to come up to Derbyshire to say goodbye. But I got a telegram when I was in London, so that was that."

There are telephones, she thought, but wisely kept silent.

"In any case," he went on, "I'm a restless character, I always told you that, too."

"With a girl in every port?" The lightness did not quite come off.

"You don't find many girls in the ports I visit. No, there's only been one girl I really missed, one I wanted to see again at all costs. She came from a small town in Derbyshire. Believe me or not, Jo, it's the truth."

She did not question it, she did not want to question it. It was enough that he was here. Reluctantly, they made their way back to the house.

Just below the steps of the verandah Bruce stopped. "How am I going to see you, Jo? Sixty miles in this country is a hell of a way to pop in on your girl. Besides, I can't impose on Neil for too long."

"But you could come over here for a stay, couldn't you?" Jo said slowly.

His face changed. "That's a terrific idea. This is one of the areas I want to cover anyway. And I'm more or less self-sufficient—I've got a Land-Rover and a tent. I'm used to living rough. Oh, lord, Jo, I can think of nothing better."

"Nor I," she said softly. "But I will have to ask Ross."

"Why? I thought this was yours and Sally's place. He's only the manager, isn't he? He looked a surly devil."

"Oh, he's all right when you get to know him. Just not very sociable. And touchy. At least I'll mention it—not ask—and to Sally, of course." She touched his arm. "Leave it to me, Bruce. There's a little matter of a truck that will decide things."

"O.K., we'll do it your way." He bent swiftly and kissed her again. "It's going to seem a long lunch. After nothing but Africans and sweating engineers, you're the most marvellous sight in the world."

Sally glanced at her sister, flushed, eyes glittering, not even trying to conceal her triumphant happiness.

Ross was handing Bruce his tall glass of beer and saying in his least welcoming tone of voice, "Neil was telling me you're prospecting in these parts. Are there any mineral deposits? Surely not."

"I'm only interested in diamonds." Bruce was drinking, sizing the other man up as if already aware of that cool, cool current.

"Diamonds around here? Impossible !"

"With diamonds you can never tell," Bruce returned calmly. "A fool's errand or not it's usually worth investigating. I've been over prospecting beyond the salt-pan where they've got a fairly big operation mounted. Now the largest find of industrial diamonds has been made just to the north, in Orapa. So for me it's time to move on. I happened to be with an old Bushman who talked about the minerals he had seen in the north. Oh, no, he hadn't seen diamonds, that would be too much to hope for, but he had studied the anthills and swore there were garnets and ilmenites."

Jo frowned, puzzled. "Anthills? What on earth have they got to do with diamonds?"

"A surprising amount. The ants bore quite deeply into the ground and if in the deposits they bring up there are those two minerals, garnets and ilmenites, it's just a chance there could be a diamond pipe. Whether the Bushman knew what he was talking about I don't know, but it's my job to find out."

The lunch Sally had organised was almost as good as any she could produce in England—with all the shops there to rely on. There was some kind of chilled fish to start with in a spicy sauce, then some chicken done as only Sally knew how to, baked with lemon juice and with a variety of unknown vegetables. The dessert was a fruit compôte in liqueur.

Quite obviously Ross simply could not believe he was in his own home. When the second course came up he looked towards Sally. "I know you said you were going to look

75

after the domestic arrangements, but I didn't realise you meant a feast like this. I think I'm worrying," he added wryly, "rather unnecessarily about probable visitors."

Neil Brand looked towards him with raised eyebrows. "Do I guess you're going to open up Nyala after all?"

"I've been bullied into it—at least to thinking about it. But before we go a step further we'll get some advice from you, Neil."

"Me? I'm afraid I can't be much help. I'm just a good old-fashioned farmer who knows how to breed cattle, not entertain tourists."

"But Ross says you have a brother," Jo put in eagerly, "who arranges small safaris. Sally and I have worked out that we could cope with a party of six to eight . . ."

"Six," Ross put in firmly.

"Well, six, then. But do you think it's too . . . too primitive here for tourists?"

"Not if they get fed like this." Neil Brand's smile was warm with admiration for Sally. He was a weathered, stocky man with bushy brown hair and a quiet, easy personality. He was the sort of man who would not speak often, but when he did people would listen.

He looked thoughtful for a moment. "My brother is always telling me that for every place there is the right tourist. There are many people who think the Kruger has been spoilt now by too much commercialisation. They'd rather make the trek to Chobe—and that's some trek. But a private reserve might be quite a temptation. I can't think there would be any difficulty at all over parties of that size. As long as you didn't oversell the facilities of Nyala. I'll have a word with my brother anyway. In fact I'll be seeing him next week. I'm off on a short business trip to the Transvaal. Sandy's coming along too."

Sandy looked at his father beseechingly. "Oh, Dad, you said you'd think about letting me stay. I could do some of your job, I know I could."

"I know you could, son, but a week is too long to be left to your own devices in this part of the world."

Sandy looked mutinous, but said nothing. His father added, "He loathes trips to town, and I really don't blame him, but our farm's nearly as isolated as this place."

"If . . . if it would help," Sally said tentatively, looking first at Ross, then at Jo, "he could come here and I could keep an eye on him. I shall be around the house most of the time . . ."

"Oh, Dad, please say yes!" The boy's eyes were alight with excitement. "I'd be ever so good and no trouble to anyone," he added virtuously, holding his breath tightly, waiting for the verdict.

Neil hesitated a moment, but obviously could not resist the utter longing in his son's face. "Well, all right, Sandy, as far as I'm concerned you can stay, as long as it's all right with Ross too." And when Ross nodded faintly, "But you've got to do exactly what Ross tells you when you're outside and what Sally and Jo tell you when you're in the house.

With a great whoop Sandy had flung himself on Goldie's prostrate form in the corner. "Just think," he cried ecstatically, "a whole week with Goldie! I've never been here for more than a weekend. Do you think we could . . ."

"Sandy," said Neil sharply, "enough of you for the moment, there are plans to make. To start with I'm not sure how we're going to get you back here. I'm catching the evening plane tomorrow."

"I could bring him," Bruce put in quietly, "the following day, if you like—Tuesday. I should probably be pulling out then anyway." He grinned. "I don't want to outstay my hospitality, Neil." Then he was looking across at Jo, telling her silently that here was her chance to invite him to stay too. But she did not respond. She must choose her moment for that . . . get Sally on her

77

side before she dropped the idea casually to Ross. Peace had been won at Nyala; there was no reason to throw it away unnecessarily.

After a leisurely lunch the party split up, Sally to take Sandy to meet Holly and Ross and Neil to the stables to look over the horses. Jo and Bruce made a pretence of following them, but Bruce pulled her away towards the shade of the river.

"You are going to fix it, aren't you?" he insisted.

"Of course, but after you've gone. There's so much to be done here, so I've got to convince Sally I'm not going to fritter away my time with you. And Ross . . . he's difficult enough anyway; I don't want him to think I'm filling the house with my friends. Everyone who comes here must be seen to have a job. He doesn't like visitors."

"I could see *that* at a glance. Don't forget what I told you before lunch, Jo, he is just the manager."

"And we can't manage Nyala without him. We're dependent on him and he knows it. Honestly, Bruce, I want you to come and stay here more than anything else at the moment, but so much rests on us making a success of Nyala that I daren't risk offending Ross Andrews. He threatened to walk out three days ago."

"Well, you don't exactly endear me to him, I must say. Still," he drew her close to him, "I suppose you know what you're doing. I reckon from what Neil said that your uncle was a bit of a character too. Did this legacy come as a real surprise?"

"I didn't even know we had an uncle in Africa, much less that he owned a game reserve. But whether it will ever be ours is another matter. It looks almost impossible."

"Who says that? Andrews?"

"And the solicitor. And our own common sense," she said ruefully, "but as long as Ross is willing to help us have a go, then I hope we have a slender chance."

"And does he want you to keep Nyala?"

She shook her head slowly. "Not really. He thinks the Government would make a much better job of looking after the place. I daresay he's right, but at least we've managed to convince him that it simply wouldn't be fair if we didn't try to face the challenge."

They met the others behind the house where Sandy was getting to know Holly. Holly was able to stand without too much wobble and she was now out of her cage, a little nervous, but more curious than anything else at the people around her. She seemed to be examining each one of them in turn. Then as though, suddenly, she had decided exactly where she was going she turned in Jo's direction, tried to run and crashed in a heap at Jo's feet.

Since only her dignity was hurt they all laughed, and as Jo eased her gently to her feet Ross reminded her : "I told you she would regard you as being completely responsible. She's yours, Jo, whether you want her or not."

"I'll help you next week," Sandy offered. "I'd like to look after her too. Goldie and I could take her for walks."

The idea of a lion, a fawn and a small boy taking walks together seemed faintly incongruous to Jo, but she nodded with due seriousness. "Of course I'd be glad of your help, Sandy."

At the river she and Sally were asked to point out where they had seen the crocodile. Neil bent to examine the bank for spoor. "There's one here all right, probably its mate as well. I just hope there aren't any young." He rose and nodded towards Ross. "When I come to collect Sandy in a week or so I'll bring my gear and we'll make a night of it. Want to come?" He smiled at Sally, who shivered slightly.

"What? Hunting crocodiles? I'd be scared out of my wits!"

"It was a big one, then?"

"Enormous!" Sally and Jo spoke in a chorus and did not understand when both men laughed.

Then Neil explained. "They all look enormous the first time, but a real crocodile-hunter will discard anything under ten feet. Up in the Okavango swamps you'll find the killers up to about eighteen feet—nasty brutes to attack you on a dark night."

"And you actually *like* hunting crocodiles?" Sally sounded appalled.

He nodded. "To me it's the greatest sport, just like to another a good tiger hunt is. Crocs are wily creatures, and you can only get them at night. You wait until those red eyes are a few feet away and then aim for the brain—the smallest of targets. You can't just shoot anywhere, because apart from the fact you probably won't kill the beasts, you'll also ruin the skin. It's only the under-belly skin that is used to make your handbags and shoes."

Jo listened, interested by what he was saying, then looked down into the calm clear waters of the river. How impossible it should be harbouring one or more crocodiles.

"And to think," she said aloud, "I was going to ask a couple of days ago whether one could swim in the river!"

"You can," said Ross calmly.

"Oh, *no*! Never!"

"But yes. Three hundred yards downstream there's a deepish pool, a natural circle formed by the rocks. When Sandy's here next week we'll show you that the crocodiles couldn't squeeze past the entrance. The most that will nudge your legs will be a couple of bream."

But still she shook her head firmly, not to be shaken even by Sandy, who told her seriously: "It's quite all right, Jo, really it is. I've swum there a lot and I've never seen a crocodile. In fact I haven't very often seen one at all, have I, Dad?" And when his father agreed he added,

"But he has promised to take me hunting in Okavango when I'm twelve."

There was no more time for Bruce and Jo to be alone, but there was Tuesday to look forward to, and perhaps more than that; for she was determined that he should stay at Nyala as long as he wanted to. Suddenly the year he had been away seemed no time at all. There had been no awkwardness, no gap to bridge. And she felt exactly the same about him as she had done at home.

But there was still Sally to face and she hated quarrelling with Sally.

After the visitors had left well before dark the two sisters walked up the steps together. "Well, Sal," said Jo lightly, "you certainly impressed us all with your cooking. What *was* that meat, anyway?"

Sally's eyes gleamed. "If I told you it was warthog you'd never trust me again, so I'm not going to tell you!"

"It wasn't really warthog, was it?" Jo grimaced.

"No," said Sally with a sweet smile, "but I believe it's excellent grilled."

"Oh," said Jo weakly, "I think I'll stick to lamb chops."

". . . Which is one thing you won't get round here." At the door to Jo's bedroom Sally blocked the way. "Well," she said quietly, "that was very well manoeuvred."

"What was?" Jo said belligerently.

"Oh, Jo, you know perfectly well. Bruce Farley's arrival."

Jo swung round on her passionately. "I swear I didn't know he was coming. How could I, Sal?"

"I don't know," Sally sighed, "but I do know you were determined to see him while you were in Africa."

"But I didn't even know where to start looking. Of course I wanted to see him, but I have enough dignity not to go chasing after someone who doesn't want me. Anyway, it was more or less a coincidence. You can ask

81

Neil if you like." And she proceeded to tell Sally how Bruce had arrived at Nyala today. At the end she added, with a trace of coldness in her voice, "You still don't believe me, do you?"

"Yes, I believe you, Jo. You never have lied."

"But you don't like Bruce any more than you liked him in England?"

"I don't dislike him. I just don't want you to fall in love with him. You'll end up by being hurt."

"How can you possibly know that?" Jo cried. "You're acting as if you were a disapproving mother or something. I suppose it's because Bruce doesn't fit into any nice neat category. He's a wanderer; he has no settled job. I know all that, and I accept it. *Someone* has to do the sort of job he's doing."

"Maybe," said Sally inexorably. "I just wish he hadn't come, that's all. I have a feeling in my bones."

"You'll be telling me next you'd rather I fell for the boorish Mr. Andrews!"

"You're hardly likely to do that, but at least I trust him. He does say exactly what he means."

"Thank you *very* much!" Jo's voice was beginning to quiver. She knew she was at that awful point, half way between temper and tears. "Well, I'll tell you one thing, Sal, when Bruce comes back here with Sandy he's coming with all his gear. I've told him he can stay at Nyala."

"You've told him what?" Sally was aghast. "I thought we were here to make Nyala pay, not to entertain your boy-friends."

Jo flushed. "That's very unfair, Sal, and you know it. I want Nyala to be a success as much as you do, if not more. I think Bruce can help. After all Ross keeps saying how short-handed he is. To start with, Bruce has got another Land-Rover, and if he wants to prospect here, he's got to do something in return, hasn't he?"

For a moment Sally was silent. "Well, we'll have to talk it over with Ross."

"Ross Andrews is nothing more than the manager here," Jo said cruelly. "Nyala belongs to *us*—or at least it might do."

Sally looked at her with something like sorrow in her eyes. "I'm sorry to have to say it, Jo, but Nyala was left to Alan and myself. We would be sharing it with you."

"Oh, God, Sal, I am a fool. I'm sorry, really I am. I just didn't think, that's all. Nyala isn't mine, is it? It never will be."

Legally, no, but in every other way, yes." Sally put her arm round her sister's shoulders. "Look, Jo, all this started over Bruce Farley. If you want him to come, then come he must. I can't bear to see you unhappy. After all, I can't spend my life looking over your boyfriends and approving them. Let's wipe out this whole conversation, and I promise to try to put all my reservations about Bruce right out of my head and pretend I'm meeting him for the first time next week. But . . ."

"Yes?" said Jo warily.

"Well, there is one thing—Ross. You're probably saying to yourself that once Bruce is here we can manage without him, but that isn't true. We need him if we're to have a hope in making something of Nyala in such a short time. He's more than just a manager. He's warden here. He runs Nyala. So we must do him the courtesy of asking him if he minds Bruce coming."

"And if he does?" Jo challenged.

"He won't if you ask him the right way. Oh, Jo, please, be just a little charitable."

Ross shrugged when Jo said that Bruce would like to come to Nyala for a short stay. "Of course I don't mind. This is your home for the time being, as well as mine. But I don't think he really imagines he'll find diamonds here, does he?"

"He seems to think there's a possibility. Ross, he could be very useful to us all. He knows the country well; he has a truck. When I told him how important Nyala was to us he said he would do anything he could to help."

"Then that's all that matters," Ross said dryly.

In the short time they had been at Nyala Jo tried to work out what made Ross Andrews such an unapproachable man. One minute he was gentling an animal back to health, the next he was as prickly as a porcupine. Sally seemed able to relax with him. She could not. And yet already she grudgingly admitted he was good at his job, and she had always respected people of ability. If only he didn't regard her with that faint look of contempt all the time! It didn't apply to Sally. Already he treated her as an equal.

On the Tuesday Bruce and Sandy were expected, she watched Ross mount his horse, Brandy, call for Tau and ride off into the bush without looking back. The three of them were like a tight-knit family—a working family. For just a moment she was full of envy at such self-sufficiency. She wished she had asked Ross if she could ride into the bush one day. The day she did that would be the day she made a great stride in earning Ross Andrews' respect. It was strange that while she did not care for him as a person it seemed important that he did not think her a fool. Sally had shown that she could take care of her end of the plans for Nyala. Now she, Jo, had to do the same.

During the morning she and Sally started to plan in detail for a minimum of six guests. Saku and the other boy turned out the three thatched rondavels and scrubbed and hosed the interiors, until they steamed in the sun. Already Sally had investigated the storerooms of the house and found spare mattresses and decided they could furnish without too much difficulty. The main thing missing was colour.

"We need," she announced, "some bright cotton for curtains and bedspreads. But where can we possibly find them? I've been all over the house, but it's too spartan to be of much use." Then Sally, ever resourceful, involved Saku in the problem, made him understand what she wanted and returned in triumph.

"He says," she told Jo, "that there's a native village about twenty miles from here and they hold a market once a week. We should be able to buy material there. That's when," she added, "we should be able to make use of Bruce Farley. He can drive one of us over at the end of the week."

The other thing Sally put in motion was the beginning of a vegetable garden. A patch was chosen not too far from the river and the gardener asked to turn over the earth ready for planting. "When we go to that market," Sally continued, "we're going to pick up every kind of seed we can. There's no reason, as long as we have enough water, why we shouldn't grow most of the things we need. And whatever we can't buy here I should be able to send away for to Johannesburg."

Jo smiled at Sally's enthusiasm. She had no doubts at all that within a very short time, Nyala would have a flourishing vegetable garden. Sally always had had the knack of making anything grow.

Suddenly Jo felt rather useless. She could take orders with the best and up to a point she was quite happy helping Sally, but her real job was to learn about the bush, how the game were scattered, what to look for, so that in the end she could share some of the trekking with Ross and Kari and even more important, that she could take a truck load of visitors on a day's safari.

After lunch, when she had rested for an hour, she wandered to the back of the house. She took a willing Holly for a walk, tickled Goldie's stomach as she passed her dozing under the trees and then found herself at the stable. The grey mare standing there looked gentle enough for anyone to ride. She hesitated only a moment, then called for Saku, indicating that she wanted the mare saddled.

Saku shook his head anxiously. "No, lady, no. *Morena* is not here."

"Is there something wrong with the horse?" Jo asked. "I mean is he dangerous to ride?"

"Oh, no, but *Morena* would not like it."

"To hell with *Morena*," Jo said under her breath. "Please see that she is saddled, Saku," she said calmly, "I am not going far. *Morena* would not mind."

He raised his hands helplessly, but went to find the garden boy, who produced a saddle and bridle while she changed into old jeans and a wide-brimmed hat.

The mare was certainly docile and she felt at home almost as soon as she was in the saddle. She had no worry about her riding ability, for as a child she had spent many weekends trekking over the Peak District. Her only doubt was being able to cope with the heat and the unknown terrain.

She did the circumference of the garden area twice, walking to get the feel of the mare, and as she looked round she saw to her amazement that wherever she went, Saku followed. Eventually she stopped.

"Why are you following me, Saku?" she demanded.

"*Morena* would wish it, lady."

"Well, you can stop it immediately. I'm perfectly all right."

He bowed his head and stood still, but when she started off again he was still plodding along behind.

Annoyed now, she dug in her heels and the mare started to trot. That would show him. She finally turned round in triumph and saw to her utter amazement that he was bent low over a bicycle, the dust flying behind him.

Jo pulled the mare round sharply. Two could play at that game! Seconds later she too was crouched in the saddle and the mare was galloping as though the devil himself were behind her. Jo almost laughed aloud. This was marvellous! She gloried in the sense of freedom as the mare galloped on, certain of its destination.

She finally slowed it down when both of them were running with sweat, patting the neck and talking easily. What a pity Ross could not see her now. Feeling enormously pleased with herself, she shaded her eyes against the glare of the sun and looked back the way she had come. There was not one track but two. She turned again and saw a third stretching into the opposite direction. Which one had she come along? The first faint twinges of alarm crept up her spine. There was no sign of the house, not even a landmark she could recognise.

Patting the mare's neck again, she said softly, "Home," and obediently the animal trotted off. But where? she wondered a few moments later. She could still be going in entirely the wrong direction.

The track she was on went in a steep curve anyway.

A sound in the bush made her jump and from almost under the horse's hooves an ugly squat animal raced across their path. She yelped in alarm, then strove for calm again. That was a warthog, but what if it had been a lion or a cheetah? Her mouth was suddenly dry as she remembered she was not just slightly lost, but in the middle of an area thick with game—some of it dangerous.

As if to emphasise that she was not alone, several buck fled along the track, followed a few seconds later by a small herd of impala. Jo was suddenly intensely aware of her vulnerability. She did not know whether her mount could outrun anything, or whether even she would care to put it to the test.

She swallowed, her throat dry from fear and from the dust of the track. She could not stay here until dusk, so once again she started off, hoping she had guessed right at the direction of the sun. Suddenly the bush was no longer friendly but alien, full of unseen enemies.

She must have been riding for fifteen minutes before she was certain she was travelling in the wrong direction. By now, surely the house would have been in sight. But she could see nothing on the horizon but two lines of trees. *One* of those must be the river. She decided on the one to her left and cut away from the track towards it.

As she urged the mare into a trot she heard the thunder of hooves behind her. This time she did not dare look, but dug in her heels. Now they would see how fast she could go.

The voice slowed her finally and when she ventured a swift turn she saw the other horse behind her.

Ross's voice was savage in its command. "Stay where you are, Jo. Don't move another step!" And she felt real fear gathering like a tight ball in her stomach.

Seconds later his hand was on her bridle. "Move one inch further and it will be the end of both of us."

CHAPTER SIX

SHE did not know how long they both waited there, immobile, the brassy sun beating down so fiercely that even the hat she wore seemed an intolerable burden. She could feel the sweat gathering between her shoulder-blades and her hands were slippery on the reins. She did not dare to turn and look at him, certain that even the slightest movement would bring down some fearful disaster.

The wait was interminable, then finally came the merest whisper in her ear. "All right, we're turning, but stay close to me and walk. Don't trot, or canter, or anything, unless I give the order. Is that understood?"

Mutely she nodded.

A few minutes later they came to a small clump of wild fig trees, frightening away two giraffe. There he reined Brandy in gently and she followed suit. By then some of her courage had returned, so had her annoyance at his high-handed treatment of her.

"All right," she rounded on him in a low, fierce voice, "now perhaps you would explain yourself. First your servant chases me on a bicycle, then you go on at me as if I were some kind of halfwit. I can't think what possible kind of harm I was doing a stone's throw from the house."

"All right, Miss Know-all, just point and tell me in which direction the house is."

"Why should I?"

"Because you tell me you're only a stone's throw from it, and because you seem anxious to persuade me you're not a . . . halfwit."

She shut her eyes, prayed, and pointed vaguely over to the left.

"So I was right; you were lost. You hadn't the faintest idea where you were. Had you gone on in the direction you were going, if you hadn't killed yourself in a particularly nasty way, you would have gone straight out into the desert."

She was silent. Perhaps he was right in some measure, but he had a particularly unfortunate way of putting over his point.

"I know you think I'm treating you like a child," he went on patiently, "but in one short trip you've made just about every mistake in the book. And by the way, don't throw the blame on Saku, he had strict instructions from me to take care of you and Sally as if you were his own children. To him that was a sacred trust. Can you imagine what he's feeling like now, knowing that he has broken that trust? He'll be holding himself completely responsible and whatever I say to him in consolation when I return will mean nothing, because his standard is higher than yours or mine."

"All right," she said flatly, "you've succeeded in making me feel like a worm. Could we go back now, even though you haven't told what the nasty death was that you've apparently saved me from."

He gave a short, dry laugh. "You still don't believe me, do you? You think, because of the winning ways of Goldie and little Holly, that this really is a sort of pets' corner. Out there, only a few yards from where you were, is a wounded buffalo. With the possible exception of a rhino it can be one of the most dangerous and unpredictable beasts in the bush. It has a hatred of the hunter, and while a herd will leave him alone, a single wounded buffalo will turn that hunter into the hunted. It will wait in ambush for him and if necessary double back on its tracks so that he hasn't the faintest idea where it will spring from. Brandy loathes buffalo, but is so well trained that he'll obey me instantly. Your mare, Betsy, would undoubtedly panic unless she felt you were perfectly in command. Now do you understand what I'm trying to say?"

She nodded slowly. "Where...where is the buffalo now?"

"Probably where it was ten minutes ago. I've seen no movement from that direction."

"Will you leave it there?"

"Of course not. That's one of the first rules of the bush—never leave a wounded animal. I've been stalking it for the past hour. It was only by chance I saw you. I imagine the poachers have had a go at it. That's the trouble with them, their shooting is simply not accurate enough. Here, you must be able to kill with a single bullet."

He pulled out his gun from its pocket in the saddle and checked the barrel. Then he turned to her and his expression had softened slightly.

"If I want to get it before dusk, then I haven't time to take you back and come out here again. I want you to wait here, Jo, and please, *don't move.* You'll be perfectly safe, but if the worst comes to the worst," he added dryly, "you can always hop up the tree. If you hear a single shot you'll know that I've found it. I'll then fire three more in rapid succession and you can come and join me. If you don't hear them, then wait for me."

"I'll wait," she said quietly, "but...but isn't it very dangerous for you to go out after it?"

"Only if I'm careless. This is what I'm paid for at Nyala—the protection of the game." Then he was trotting away, directly into the sun.

She watched him go, straining her eyes after him as he slowed to a cautious walk. Only now did she feel ashamed of such foolhardy behaviour. She had acted quite without thought for herself or others—something she did far too often, according to Sally.

In spite of the shade from the trees it was still

breathlessly hot. How long, she wondered, would she have to wait here, straining for that shot?

In the still air it seemed that nothing moved, except a small brightly coloured bird that darted in and out of the leaves above her head. She tried to concentrate her thoughts on Bruce, who would surely have arrived by now with Sandy. Certainly, both he and Sally would have learned of her flight from Saku, so there would be no hope of hiding her foolishness.

It was going to be good to have Bruce here. Her heart warmed at the thought of him. At least he treated her like a reasonable adult. Bruce knew both the bush and the desert. From him perhaps she could learn not to make the same mistakes twice. Rather from him than Ross, who would make an uncompromising teacher. Even now, she could feel the lash of his sarcasm.

As Ross returned to her thoughts she began to wonder why there had been no shot. The hunted turned into the hunter, he had said. Was there any reason why, however careful he was, he should consider himself invincible? She suddenly pictured him lying there kicked and gored . . . and she would not even know.

That earlier, insidious fear crept back into her bones. She did not want to move, or disobey his instructions, but how long would he expect her to stay there? Darkness could not be too far away and it would come without warning. The thought of being out here at night when all the beasts of prey came out to hunt and prowl was a fearsome thought.

Suddenly the sound of a shot echoed on the still, hot air. Dry-mouthed, she waited for the next three. When they did not come immediately, the gruesome picture returned to her mind. So he had missed that single, vital shot. He must have done . . .

When the signal finally came she could have wept with relief and she urged Betsy into a canter over the thick sandy scrub.

Ross emerged from the cover of some bushes, unmounted, waving at her with his rifle. When she reached him he said, "You'd better come and have a look. You won't often see a dead buffalo."

She looked down at the huge beast, rock-like in size, with its horns looking like something out of an ancient picture book. Seeing it lying there so peacefully it was hard to imagine death waiting at the end of those vicious horns.

"It seems suddenly sad," she said soberly.

"It always is when an animal has to die this way," he answered. "The buffalo is intelligent and cunning. It can be schemingly vindictive, but it's also a proud beast."

He bent suddenly and with a swift movement hacked off the tail which he wrapped up as casually as if it were some kind of belt and stuffed it in his saddle bag.

"A trophy?" she could not resist asking.

"No," he replied calmly, "tomorrow's lunch, probably. Buffalo makes almost as good a stew as oxtail, or even better, probably, if your sister supervised it."

She wrinkled up her nose distastefully. It was one thing not to know what you were eating, quite another to see it freshly killed. She had never before seriously considered how the oxtail she so enjoyed in England started out at home.

She wheeled her horse round. "I'm sure you're right. Are we going back now?"

He nodded. "Yes. You must be very tired and very hot, I imagine."

"A little," she admitted, "but I think I'm going to get along with the climate far better than I expected. And, Ross ..." she paused.

"Yes?"

"I want to apologise to Saku. Will he really blame himself as you said?"

"I'm afraid so. He's rather an emotional fellow, quite

unlike Kari, who would regard it as a mark of weakness to show what he was feeling. But he'll understand an apology and accept it. The only thing is . . . and I warn you . . . he'll be even more vigilant in future."

"Oh, well, I suppose I deserve it." It was the nearest she could come to apologising to him.

"And, Jo . . ."

"In the middle of all my criticism there's one compliment I can pay you."

She turned sharply towards him, expecting sarcasm, but finding only an oddly serious expression on his lean face. "You ride like a professional. Did you learn when you were a child?"

"Yes. My father was quite a well-known amateur rider. He entered for most of the local races. He taught us all almost as soon as we could walk. Sally was never quite so keen as Alan and myself. Dad used to take us trekking over the Peaks for a day when we were young, then for a weekend when he thought we could manage it. Those were good times," she smiled rather sadly, suddenly remembering her father, "but I haven't ridden very much during the past few years."

"I said I would take you out in the Land-Rover for a longish day. I'll do the same on horseback if you think you can take it. It's the finest way to learn bushlore there is. You'll need to know how to find your way by the sun, how to recognise landmarks. But I warn you now, this is only if you really want to reach the heart of Nyala. It will be no picnic and I'm a hard taskmaster. I won't be thinking of you as a girl visiting the reserve, but one of my own trainee rangers."

"I'd like to do that," she said truthfully. "Whatever you may think, I want to learn about Nyala more than anything else. I told you before that the domestic arrangements are definitely Sally's province. This is where I want . . . Oh, look Ross, isn't that a truck ahead kicking up all that dust?"

"I imagine," he said dryly, "your friend Bruce Farley is sending out a search party for you."

She flashed an angry look at him. "You sound just like Sally—sarcastic whenever Bruce is mentioned. Has she been trying to influence you?"

"I make my own judgements about people, Jo, and," he pointed out, "I have only met your Mr. Farley over one lunch. Hardly time to form an opinion."

"Sally formed her opinion in as short a time as that," she responded with some bitterness.

The truck reached them and pulled up with a squeal of brakes. Bruce leaned out anxiously. "Are you all right Jo? Saku is wringing his hands and wailing back there ... something about a runaway horse. And now Sally is in a real state too."

"I'm fine." Jo tried to keep her voice light. "And I'm sorry to have thrown everyone into a stew. Did you have a good trip, Bruce, and is Sandy with you?"

"Yes, he wanted to come, but Sally said 'no' very firmly." He grinned. "I really believe your sister was imagining the worst. I must say you look a bit tired, Jo, do you want a lift back?"

"No." But Ross already had his hand on her bridle.

"I think it would be a good idea for you to go with Farley. We're farther away than you think."

"No, really, I can't," she protested, but torn between not wanting to give in and wanting to be with Bruce. "What about Betsy?"

"Betsy would follow Brandy into the middle of the Kalahari—and beyond."

Half reluctantly Jo dismounted and climbed into the passenger seat. Bruce reached across her and closed the door. But he did not withdraw his hand. He kissed her gently. "You really did give us all quite a fright, you know."

Unconsciously this time she pulled away. The shadow of Ross Andrews moving off with the two horses had only just left the window. There was no need to go on proving herself to him.

He switched on the engine and started to turn the car. "What's the matter?"

"Nothing . . . I was just thinking I gave myself quite a fright too. I never realised that this was a country without landmarks."

"Oh, there are landmarks all right, but you have to learn to distinguish them. Look," he pointed out of the window, "that tree on the skyline over there. You would be able to pick that out from a range of at least two miles. It has a curious formation in its top two branches. Then here, on your left," he slowed down, "that's not a track, but it's a trail used pretty often by elephants. Only an elephant pushes over bushes in just that way. Then there are the smaller things like an oddly shaped anthill, an area which a particular animal frequents, even different formations of the land. That's what I look for."

She sighed. "You make it sound so easy."

"No. No, it's not easy; it's just what you have to learn if you're to survive in the bush. This is a harsh and unforgiving country. But it can also be rewarding, so you have to respect it."

Jo found herself relaxing in the truck. She watched the easy, relaxed way his big hands rested on the steering wheel, the way the sun picked up the golden hairs of his arms.

"You are really going to stay, aren't you?" she said suddenly.

"Oh yes," he turned towards her and his eyes were smiling behind dark glasses, "if you've all agreed to have me. Even Andrews?"

"Oh, Ross is all right, I told you that before. Anyway, he's been crying out for extra help around Nyala. He'll soon find you're not exactly going to be a parasite."

"Oh, I'll work my passage all right," he said lazily,

"only one thing really worries me."

"What's that?" she said alarmed.

"The fact of not seeing you on your own often enough. I'm not sure that I'll fit in with all this communal living. I can't even take you out to dinner."

"No, you'll have to take me out for a day in the bush instead," she teased him. "Somehow I've got to learn the dos and don'ts of bushlore if we're really going to have safari parties down here."

"I don't really know yet what your position is over Nyala, how important it is to make it pay, and what chance you've got."

"According to Ross, none at all. But Sally and I are determined to go down fighting."

"Then after the meal tonight, we'll go down to my camp and you can tell me the whole story from start to finish. I have only the bare outlines from Neil." As they drove towards the house, he squeezed her hand. "If you want to fight, Jo, then I'm going to help you."

Sandy was waiting for them dancing about on the door step with impatience. "Hello," he said politely to Jo, holding out his hand, then—much more eagerly—"Where's Ross, isn't he coming?"

"Yes, in about fifteen minutes, I should think," she told him. "He's got both Brandy and Betsy with him."

The boy looked at Bruce with faint accusation. "You could have taken me, you know, Mr. Farley, then I could have ridden Betsy back. She knows me quite well."

"I'm sorry, Sandy," Bruce apologised, "but we didn't even know Ross was out there with Jo. I daresay he'll let you ride later in the week."

Sally came out then, and stood with her hands on her hips watching her younger sister. "Where on earth . . . ?"

With a sigh, Jo interrupted, "If you're going to start telling me off, you can save your breath. Ross did that quite adequately. In fact he told me off soundly enough for two of you. I took the horse out without permission, and yes, I did try to evade Saku, and yes, I'm perfectly all right, and I'm going to apologise to him."

Sally's face softened. "Oh, Jo, you are a fool. I was just worried, that's all. It's years since you've been riding."

"Well, I haven't lost the knack," Jo said defiantly, "and now if you'll all excuse me I'm going in for a shower."

From the bathroom she heard the sound of hooves and then Sandy's voice, firing eager questions at Ross. Certainly, with the boy, he had infinite patience. He seemed better at communicating with animals and children than with adults.

When she returned to her bedroom she found she had made the mistake of leaving her door open. Of course, Goldie was curled up there snoring gently. Without thought now, Jo pushed her off and was rewarded with a reproachful look and an indignant swish of the tail. She slapped Goldie on the haunch and herself collapsed on the bed, wishing that Nyala had been able to afford air-conditioning in the bedrooms.

Only now, rested, refreshed and alone, did she begin to relive the scene of the past hour. The sight of the massive buffalo carcase returned to her, an almost prehistoric beast in its proportions. She shuddered at the thought of the damage those horns could do. If only Ross Andrews were not so insufferably bossy she could probably take his criticism, yet one tiny corner of her could not help admiring his cool walking out to face a dangerously wounded animal with such complete lack of fear.

The thought of him made her wonder idly how he would run Nyala if he were left completely on his own. A man as unsociable as he was, with no wife, no company but animals and native servants, would probably turn cranky. And it would not take too much to turn Ross Andrews cranky.

"Aren't you coming for a drink?" She opened her eyes

to find Sally watching her. "I was beginning to think you'd really fallen asleep."

"No . . . no, just a bit tired, but the shower more or less fixed that. I'll be with you in five minutes. Oh . . . and Sally?"

Her sister turned.

"Did Ross produce tomorrow's supper for you?"

She half expected her sister to grimace, but Sally nodded happily. "Yes, buffalo tail; he said it tastes as good as oxtail. And don't look like that, Jo, there isn't a butcher's shop round the corner. We'll have to make use of what we can get here. I've been reading a bit too and I reckon I'll be able to make paté for visitors. Ross has promised to save the first liver from any wildebeest. And he says that farther up the river are duck and guinea-fowl. I honestly believe we could produce a very good menu here."

Dinner that evening should have been rather in the nature of a celebration, but somehow there was an air of tension around, only saved by Bruce's cheerfulness and the eager questions of young Sandy.

Ross seemed detached; at least he hardly joined in the conversation at all, and when the meal was over and they were waiting for Saku to bring the coffee, he walked over to the window and stared down towards the river.

Sandy came over and stood beside him. "Are you looking for the croc, Ross?"

Ross ruffled his hair. "No, that's your dad's job. We're going to wait for him to come back and finish that fellow off. No, I'm worried about the water supply. We depend on the river and it's going down about an inch a day."

Sally came to join them. "Is it really bad?" she asked.

"It's never bad until the worst has happened, but we're dependent on the river. We should have more pumps at the farthest water-holes, but they're always too costly an item."

In the soft light Sally's eyes were glinting. "Should a

99

pump come before a deep-freeze?" she said demurely.

She drew from him the first smile of the evening. "It should, but a deep-freeze is cheaper. Besides, I was beginning to forget what good food is like. Now I'm fast developing a taste for it."

Jo watched the little scene by the window. She saw the way their eyes met. Sally certainly had the knack of relaxing Ross. She could even make him laugh.

Bruce's hand was resting lightly on her shoulder. "Do you want to wait for coffee, or will you have some of my own brew? It tastes good out of doors."

So they slipped away, unnoticed, down to where the river curved sharply round about two hundred yards from the back of the house. Here Bruce had organised a small but highly efficient camp site, with the truck facing the water and a small brown tent pitched beside it. The embers of a fire still glowed from the midst of a frame of small rocks. Bruce reached up and lit a storm lamp hooked above the tent. It threw into the sharper light the scene, even the folding table and two camp chairs.

Jo gazed with admiration. "You really have made it look like home!"

"Don't forget," he reminded her, "this *is* my home. I may have to be on the move and travel light, but I do enjoy a few comforts, otherwise this kind of life could grow intolerable."

"But a table . . . and chairs?"

"I need a table because I have paper work to do. And to sit at a table one needs a chair. I also have a camp bed and a sleeping bag. Now, first—coffee."

She watched him heat the water in a billy can, then measure the coffee into metal cups. She had not quite visualised Bruce in these surroundings, fending for himself, so utterly self-sufficient. When he had been in England he had fitted in so well there, his tall figure comfortable and casual in its well cut suit. He was an

Englishman home from the tropics, true, but not one from this rough sort of life.

He looked up and caught her gaze, grinning. "I know what you're thinking."

"Well, what am I thinking?"

"That I'm not your idea of a diamond prospector. The ones you've seen are at the cinema, old, wizened, grubby, with a few weeks' growth of beard on their faces. Well, things aren't like that any more, although you can still find some of the old-timers just outside Kimberley in South Africa. They look for diamonds in much the same way as they did a century ago. I don't, I look for the pipe that might hide a million pounds' worth of diamonds. Sugar?" She nodded and he handed her the mug already stirred.

"And how do you start looking on Nyala?"

She listened, absorbed as he talked of his real love, the search for diamonds. At home he had also talked a little, but it had never seemed quite so real as now, in just the sort of terrain he was describing. He told her how they sank the shafts deeper and deeper until they came to the 'blue ground', the rock that was diamond-bearing, and then they started to tunnel through the sides, parallel to the surface. He also told her of the year he had spent in South-West Africa, working on the treacherous coast there, where the slow search for sea diamonds was going on.

For a moment she realised he had almost forgotten she was there. "I'm sorry, Jo," he said ruefully, "you started me off on my pet subject. And you really listened. Most women ask questions, but don't really want to know the answers."

I want to know about you, anything.

He said suddenly: "It would solve all your problems if I found diamonds on Nyala, wouldn't it?"

She frowned, puzzled. "But how?"

"Money problems. They simply wouldn't exist. You

could even afford to keep the reserve as a private garden. You could certainly afford to get rid of Andrews."

"Do you dislike him that much?" she asked curiously.

"No, of course not. I was just pointing out facts. But I've never liked to be dependent on anyone but myself for bread and butter. You're completely dependent on him. He could so easily let you down."

"He could, but I don't think he will. He has too much pride." She thought a moment more and added, "I suppose the truth is he doesn't really want to run Nyala commercially. He would like to continue in the same way as my uncle was doing."

Bruce snorted. "Towards ruin, by the sound of it. Look, Jo," he turned to her and gripped her shoulders, "you sound as if you're not entirely happy with Andrews. Even when you praise him, there's a note of doubt in your voice. I'm not suggesting that game rangers or wardens grow on trees, but mostly they're a band of dedicated men, and you could always replace Andrews. Oh, not at a day's notice, true, but I could always get friends of mine to look around."

"No, honestly, Bruce," she said anxiously, "I don't want to run him down at his job. My only criticism is that he has a difficult personality. Just because he and I don't hit it off . . . In the end it's only the animals that count."

"The humans too, if you're going to make it pay. Anyway, let's forget him and talk about you for a change. I want to know exactly what you've done in the past year."

So she leaned her head against his shoulder in the firelight and talked. She knew that what she said to him was not particularly interesting, but it was so good to have him here and not to imagine that last year was all a dream. Even the setting was perfect; the soft glow of the fire and the shaded lamps from the house; the distant sounds of the bush she was already beginning to recognise, from the husky shout of the hyena to the barking of baboons and every few moments the faint but distinctive rumble of an elephant.

"England seems a long way away now," he said.

"Another world," she moved deeper into the shelter of his arms. "And you know, it's a funny thing, but I know three months isn't going to be long enough for me here. I feel I could be happy."

He looked down at her. "Why not? You're only trying to express what many people feel about Africa. It's still a very wild and mysterious place. And you know something, Jo?"

"What's that?"

"I had a feeling in my bones that you and I were meant to meet in Africa. That's why I knew I would see you again. There was no need to write. When you're alone as much as I am, there's time to think and there are some things in life one is quite certain of." His arms tightened round her. "This time I'm not going to let you go."

CHAPTER SEVEN

DURING the following evening Ross, in a surprisingly expansive mood, suggested he should take a busman's holiday and they would all spend the day in the bush. That the trip was mostly for Sandy was obvious, but Ross said he also wanted to make a start on Goldie's training and possibly discuss key points in the reserve that might be designated as stopping places, or viewing areas, for potential visitors.

"It won't be altogether a holiday," he apologised, "because I might have to do some work along the way and make at least one call at a game post, but we should be able to cover a fair amount of ground and see a good selection of game." He turned to Bruce. "I hope you'll come along. It will give you the feel of the place. I might even be able to help you with some of the problems of the terrain."

"And you'd like the use of my truck," Bruce finished lazily. But he was smiling as he spoke.

Ross had glanced sharply at him. "If you're coming, yes," he replied evenly. "I'd like to do the thing properly and take Kari and a couple of the boys."

Bruce shrugged. "It's all right by me. I want to do a few small engine checks, but I should be able to get that done tonight. What time are you proposing to start?"

"Five o'clock."

Sally spoke up next. "I'm not sure that I'll come, Ross. All-day travelling and I don't seem to go too well together, and I don't want to be a drag."

"You won't," he said confidently, "we're not trying to beat any time records. We'll also be making several long-ish stops, that's one of the reasons why I want the boys along, so that they can give a hand with the food. We'll also take a tent in case we're out of shade at midday. For tomorrow, Sally, we'll go at your pace, not mine."

She looked relieved. "Then I'll come, of course, or I'll find myself back in England without having seen enough game, or the other boundaries of Nyala."

"Fine. And what we will do," he added, "is to assume that you, Sally, and Jo—and Farley—are members of a day safari out from Nyala. We can then see what you would think of the facilities if you were really paying customers."

It all seemed a good idea, Jo thought, until she tumbled out of bed just after four-thirty the next morning. It was still pitch dark and the air cool and fresh, but the effort of rising after not quite enough sleep and the heavy programme of the previous days seemed enormous.

Only two people were quite wide awake, Ross and Sandy—who was dancing around the steps bubbling over with excitement. The two trucks were already out and packed, except for the last few things the boys were carrying out amid a great deal of shouting and gesticulating. Saku was not coming himself, but he was quite determined he should be held responsible for arranging everything efficiently.

At last only the human element was left. Without asking if anyone had preferences, Ross ordered them to their places.

"Sally, I think you'd better travel with Farley, along with Kari and one of the boys. You've also got the tent and a fair bit of gear in the back there. I'll take Sandy and Jo, with Goldie in the truck with the other boy."

When Jo opened her mouth to protest, his only comment was, "I daresay you'd prefer it to be the other way round, but if I'm to teach you anything about Nyala it will have to be like this." His eyes rested coolly on her mutinous expression. "You *were* intending to set yourself up as a safari leader one day, weren't you?"

Without another word Jo climbed into the truck alongside Sandy. As usual he was right, but oh, the pleasure he took in the smallest of humiliations!

He and Bruce arranged final signals between them for stopping or drawing each other's attention, then they were moving slowly off, down the main track, heading towards the south-west and the largest game post of Nyala, other than the main house.

At about five-thirty, the first pink tendrils of the dawn crept across the sky and then the light seemed to burst all about them, first a cool, soft grey, then as the sun rose turning it to gold. And with the light came the game, rising silently to make its way towards the river and the water-holes.

They were heading, Ross said, to one of the largest and most important water-holes in the south-west of Nyala, only twenty miles from the border post, almost on the edge of the real desert. Even a few days ago, he added, the water was getting dangerously low.

"Does the water ever dry up completely?" she asked curiously.

"It's never done in my time here, but it can do; and then of course all the game heads towards the river. For some it would simply be too far and they would die on the way. Without appearing to lecture you," he added dryly, "this is one of the reasons we need money so badly. If we have money we can buy pumps and if we have pumps we can at least keep some of the holes going."

Just before seven they stopped for breakfast. Within minutes the boys had put up the tent with its flat canopy and had coaxed a fire into speedy life for the water to boil. The smell of frying eggs in the sharp morning air suddenly made Jo aware that she was really hungry.

They sat round in the shade of the tent, eating and talking about the possibilities of the day ahead. Goldie seemed faintly ill-humoured for once, pushing her way into the circle and nudging Ross until he almost fell off his stool. Jo could only assume she did not like travelling, then she turned away for a second and found herself tipped off her canvas chair and sprawling on the ground.

The others all roared with laughter. Even the Africans grinned at her discomfiture.

"Wretched lion," she grumbled. "Why can't you keep her under control, Ross Andrews? She can jolly well travel in another truck."

He tickled the lioness behind her ear. She merely growled faintly.

"You see," Jo said crossly, dusting off the sand. "She got out of bed the wrong side this morning."

He shook his head, still smiling. "No, it's not that, she's hungry. At the moment she's contemplating those nice bare arms of yours."

Jo gave a little gasp. She was not used to Ross in a teasing mood. Quickly she rolled her sleeves down. "I thought you always fed her late at night."

"Yes, but not today. Today Goldie is going hunting." He shooed Goldie out of the breakfast circle. With an ill-humoured grunt she went and lay down under the dappled shade of a camel-thorn.

It was then the family of baboons seemed to appear from nowhere. Their barking could be heard over the still air and though they did not come near the breakfast camp at first their curiosity brought them closer.

"But they're so ugly," Sally breathed, watching the cluster of hairy grey beasts whose stance from a distance looked so incredibly human. "What do they want?"

"Like Goldie, a good square meal," Ross answered laconically, watching the group. "They must have broken away from the main troop, because this is certainly not their terrain."

"I don't think they're ugly," announced Jo, "they look rather friendly."

"Not baboons," Ross shook his head, "they're

mischievous, greedy, predatory animals. They have curious habits too; they move in this tight family group, yet as often as not they won't raise a finger to help one of their number in trouble. They are also extraordinarily destructive. I once mistakenly saved a young baboon from drowning and brought him home. One minute he was almost human, the next he would try to smash the place. And you want to see the troop elder in action, he behaves just like a despotic dictator."

For a few moments longer they watched the troop, who were playing like children, tearing up and down the trees, chasing each other, putting on tumbling acts like clowns.

There were quite a few young in the group, one in particular who did not appear to have much clue as to how the game was supposed to be played. He kept getting left out, wailing and crying when he did so, much to the amusement of the girls. Finally he decided the only way to be quite sure of doing right was to stay close to father. First of all he pulled on his tail and he turned on him angrily, then he climbed on to his back and clung there with all his might as the older animal raced up the nearest tree.

But suddenly laughter turned to horror. The whole scene was over in seconds. It seemed that the parent baboon did not want the child just then. He was nothing but nuisance value. First he appeared to be trying to shake the infant off its back, who clung with extra tenacity. Then, in one swift movement, in a terrifying outburst of rage, the parent lifted the encumbrance from its back, bit it hard and tossed it to the ground, forty feet below.

"Oh, no!" cried Jo, instinctively, and got up to run to where the tiny body lay sprawled beneath the trees.

"Stay where you are," snapped Ross, "they don't like interference; they could just as easily turn on you." He reached in the truck for his gun. As he walked over, the chattering in the trees died to an uneasy murmuring. But when he bent to the ground, the whole troop turned and fled, abandoning the infant.

"It's dead, I suppose," Jo said flatly when he returned. He nodded.

"I never thought the animal world was *deliberately* cruel." She was more upset by the little scene than she would have cared to admit.

"It isn't," Ross told her, "but there are animals with a bad streak just as there are humans. But you mustn't condemn them all. If that had been a young elephant calf lying there dead the herd would have come and carried it away as a sort of ritual. It's their custom. You'll see many sights in the bush that will sicken you, Jo, until you get used to them, but even more they'll fill you with wonder."

"I suppose so." But for the moment she was unconvinced, still seeing that small body hurtling through the air like a discarded football.

Bruce caught her eye. "Here, Jo, I've poured out some more tea. Drink it." And she took it from him gratefully, glad to have her attention diverted.

Young Sandy, wanting also to help, came and stood before her saying seriously, "I don't like those things either, Jo, but you do learn to get used to them. Why, I can remember on the farm when a hyena got one of Dad's cattle before it was dead. All of its guts . . ."

"Sandy," Ross's voice came sharply across the clearing, "how about collecting up Goldie before she falls completely asleep?"

Bruce grinned at Jo and squeezed her hand. "It's all right, I believe all children have strong stomachs and tend to be a bit ghoulish."

It was probably because of the baboons that Jo reacted quite so strongly to what happened only a short time later. Goldie had been reluctantly roused and Ross, picking up his gun, said to Sandy, "We're going to give her the first lessons in survival. Do you want to come, or stay here with the boys?"

"And me," Sally chimed in. "I'm not moving anywhere until I have to." Already she had stretched out under the awning, lazily watching all the preparations.

"I'd like to come, please, Ross," Sandy said eagerly, just managing to apologise to Sally. "If you don't mind, that is, Sally."

"Of course I don't mind. What about you, Jo?"

"I'm going too." Jo picked up her hat and dark glasses, looking inquiringly at Bruce, who nodded, taking her by the arm in a comforting sort of way.

So the little party started on foot across the sandy bush towards a larger patch of trees about half a mile away, with Ross in the lead accompanied by the faithful Tau and Goldie, still letting her disapproval be known by occasional unfriendly grunts, padding on just behind. Kari brought up the rear with Sandy, Bruce and Jo in the middle.

When Jo asked why they had not made their breakfast camp there Ross answered briefly: "Dunes ... just ahead. We would have had to make a detour of a couple of miles." And as they came up to the shelter of those dunes he asked them to stay as still and silent as possible.

Jo leaned against the hot dry sand. If she closed her eyes she could almost imagine she was in Cornwall, where they used to spend their holidays as children, with the great rolling dunes covered in dry, scrubby grass.

Here there was scrub, uneven and sparse, where it looked as though rain had not fallen for years, except that Bruce had already described to her the overnight blossoming of the desert when the rains did come. For a short while it became green and cascades of brilliant flowers burst out of the sand as if by magic.

They waited, although Jo was not certain why they were waiting, until she saw the small herd of impala appear just a couple of hundred yards away. They were travelling slowly, stopping every now and then to probe at half-hidden green shoots from the bush. Then, as if at a perfectly timed signal, they all lifted their heads and it seemed, in a single graceful movement, they were all leaping into the distance.

As the last animal passed their field of vision, Ross raised his rifle and fired. The impala seemed to hesitate for a second in mid-air, then fell, crumpled in a heap. The sound of the shot seemed to echo in the sudden silence of the bush.

Ross urged Goldie forward. But Goldie still seemed reluctant, hungry as she was.

Jo, bemused, was staring at Ross in utter disbelief. She found her voice at last.

"Do you mean to say you shot that ... that beautiful creature just on a whim, just so that you could give Goldie a little afternoon's fun? You're ... you're almost as bad as that baboon!"

Ross stopped in his tracks. "I think it should have been you to stay at home today, not Sally. If you think and talk that way then there's no place for you in the bush ... come on, Goldie." His voice sharpened. "We're not having another squeamish one on our hands."

But Jo had not finished. She ran after him, pulling back on his arm. "I'm not joking, Ross ... this isn't the way I want to run Nyala."

"Nyala isn't yours to run, is it?" he returned in that same cool voice. "And if your stomach won't stand even an ordinary kill, then you'd better go back to your sister. Now."

For just a few more seconds there was silence as they faced each other, anger about to explode into violence. Sandy was already pushing Goldie by the haunches towards where the impala had fallen.

Suddenly Bruce intervened. "Look," he said roughly, "I agree that that was an ill-timed piece of shooting, especially after the baboon killing. Surely you've got sense enough to see that Jo is upset?"

Ross leaned forward, resting on his gun. "Well, I did think you would have had more sense, Farley. I thought you would help me point out to Miss Fraser yet again that this isn't Kew Gardens."

"I daresay she knows that already. But it takes time to learn the ways of the desert."

"And that's just what we haven't got around here— time! At least not if I follow my instructions correctly and try to make Nyala into a paying proposition."

"And that includes slaughtering buck in front of girls?"

Although his skin was so tanned, Ross Andrews appeared to have whitened in his anger. His eyes were black coals and his mouth tight in his effort to control himself.

He turned deliberately away from Bruce and looked at Jo. "You're not a child, Jo ... where do you think the meat comes from that you eat at table every night, that Goldie eats every night, and Tau, every living thing that has to be fed on Nyala? From my gun, of course. I presume you're one of those people who know unpleasant things go on in the world, but as long as you don't actually see them you can pretend they don't exist. What about the beef and lamb you eat at home? Before you start handing out orders about what I should do, what Goldie should eat, you should become a vegetarian. At least you would be trying to stick to your principles. I suppose you'd like me to keep this lion in captivity all her life, so that she would end up in some wretched zoo, simply because no one had had the decency to teach her to feed herself. Already I've left it too long, because there's never enough damn time round here." He looked from Bruce back to Jo, then jerked his head towards Sandy. "Even a nine-year-old boy accepts the simple fact that in the bush if you want to have life there must be death." With that he strode off.

Bruce started after him. "Damned insolence ... who the devil does he think he is? I'll ..."

"No, please, Bruce." Jo restrained him. "It won't do the slightest bit of good."

"You mean to say you don't mind him speaking to you as he might one of the African servants?"

"Of course I mind." Jo did not add that she would have been very surprised if Ross had ever spoken to a servant like that. "But starting another row won't help. I suppose he's right in a way ... it's his methods I don't like."

"Shock tactics, you'd call them. He's just the cold-blooded type to do something like that deliberately, knowing how you would feel. Come on, Jo, we'll walk back to Sally." He put his arm lightly round her shoulders. "Would you like to pack up for the day and I'll drive you back? You look a little rough."

She shook her head. "No, I can't give in that easily. It's barely past breakfast time. But whatever he says I'm not driving in the truck with him. I'll change places with Sally."

Ross made no comment when the boys had packed up and he found her already seated beside Bruce. He merely said, "We'll keep heading south-west to the water-hole, but there's not much of a track, so we'll have to take it slowly. We should then get to the post in time for lunch." He added curtly to Jo, "Watch out for kudu ... great shy beasts, usually found alone, and if you're lucky you might also see roan antelope. This is their part of the country, not to mention lion—wild lion. It will be Goldie's first meeting with her own species, if we see any."

"I expect Bruce will be able to identify them for me!" Jo answered stiffly.

When they had been following the leading truck for a few miles—some distance behind because of the dust clouds—Bruce turned to her and said: "Do you really believe Ross Andrews intends to try and make the place pay for you?"

She hesitated. "I don't really know, we just have to rely on him. I know you think it's foolish, Bruce, but we have no alternative. Sometimes I think Sally and I are living in a fool's paradise."

"Not if we can get even a whiff of diamonds." He gripped her arm tightly. "No, Jo, it's not as impossible as all that. These Bushmen have an uncanny knack of being right. There's no logic, just instinct. Tomorrow I'm going to start work in earnest. You might not see me for two or three days at a time, but I'll never be more than twenty or thirty miles away. The more self-sufficient I am the better. I'll only need to come to the house for water . . . and to see you."

"I'm glad you came, Bruce," she said, "somehow you make everything seem possible." She looked out at the passing countryside, mile after mile of flat, sandy scrub that looked as though it could not sustain a living thing. "I don't want to go back to England," she said suddenly. "Even if Nyala falls about our ears, I don't think I want to go back yet."

"Then stay," his hand was still gripping hers. "There are other parts of Africa, other countries as interesting as this one. But you're not to give up hope yet, Jo. With well over two months to go you and I are going to get this place buzzing."

"Oh, Bruce," she sighed, "I only hope you're right." But even as she spoke she had a curious feeling of disloyalty towards Ross Andrews.

In about an hour they reached the water-hole. Somehow Jo had expected a kind of miniature lake, or even a pan—one of the indents in the ground found all over the country, mostly dried up, some layered with salt, occasionally with mud or a couple of feet of water— but this was less than a small village pond.

In its own way, Jo saw as she climbed out of the truck, it was quite pretty, rather like finding a green oasis in the middle of a desert. Round the edges of the hole grew a coarse kind of grass, much trampled by animals trying to reach the diminishing water. There were also small clumps of trees, the first they had seen for the past hour. She heard Ross explaining to Sally that although the water area was small, normally enough filtered through the ground to give life to the game within ten miles, and in the hollows where the water collected seeds were blown and in the short wet season the trees sprang up, giving shelter and shade and a nesting area for the birds.

Ross pushed his hat to the back of his head and knelt to examine the hole, but with his hand he scooped out only moisture along with the desert sand.

He looked up at Kari who was anxiously standing by and shook his head. "It is bad, *Morena*," Kari replied solemnly. "In two days there will be nothing."

"And there's not a damn thing we can do about it." He looked angrily up into the brazenly blue sky as if seeking for some small sign of rain.

There was an air of faint depression over all of them as they moved back towards the trucks. Then the first of the morning visitors came to drink and they drew back silently to watch. First came the springbok and a small herd of wildebeest. They drank together, yet stayed apart. In a low voice Ross explained to Sally and Sandy that there was an unwritten drinking order to some of these scattered holes. The different species came in a regular order.

As the springbok drew back four or five warthog rushed down to the water, scrambling over each other in their haste to reach the moisture.

Then came the zebra, but even as they took their place their eyes went up sharply as though the scent of danger was there and they could not understand it.

"It's Goldie," explained Ross. "They can smell lion when it's not really time for the lion. The lion comes last, after the rest of the buck."

And so it turned out to be. Jo watched the pride stroll down to water, a magnificent lion, shaggy-maned, the lioness and several younger ones. There must have been about eight in all. And as they came the rest of the game disappeared as if by magic.

Ross pushed Goldie forward, but she took one look at her fellow beasts and yelped in fright, running round to cower at the far side of the truck. She had come across something she simply did not understand.

"Why," breathed Sandy, "she's frightened, Ross, honestly I think she is!"

"I'm afraid you're right," Ross replied gravely. "Just one more lesson for her to learn. She's not proving to be much good as a pupil today." He turned to Sally, explaining, "She'd never even seen a fresh kill earlier on. She didn't know what to do with it. She's grown indecently tame."

When the last of the animals had gone Kari and Ross returned to the hole, shovelling into the sand all around it, but there was no spread of moisture and Ross finally threw his shovel down in disgust, sweat pouring off him with the effort he had made.

They all stood in a group watching him, the African boys a little apart, but with the same expressions of sympathy on their faces, all wanting to help, but equally knowing that anything said just now would be merely frivolous.

He seemed to see them for the first time and, as if they were all his servants, barked out : "Right, into the trucks, there's nothing we can do here."

Bruce backed his truck out after the other one, slamming the gears home. "This is turning out to be a fine safari, isn't it? I don't give your Ross Andrews much chance of pleasing the tourists if he takes his bad temper out on them—or worse still treats them all like a bunch of school kids."

"I suppose he's worried," Jo said helplessly. "The drought must be getting serious."

"I daresay, but a good warden would have made some provision for an eventuality like this. A drought is always on the cards in this part of the country."

"Oh, Bruce, that isn't fair," she protested. "Heaven knows I'm annoyed enough with him today, but he's only been in charge of Nyala for a month or two. The only thing he could have done was to put in pumping equipment—and that takes money."

He smiled wryly down at her. "O.K., Jo, you have a kind heart and I don't. It's just that the fellow gets under my skin. But you know, if you're going in for the tourist business seriously, you'll have to think whether he's the right man for it. I feel he's going to rub a lot of people up the wrong way."

Jo did not answer. He was right about this. The thought depressed her.

She looked out at the unending vista of sand and more sand and knew that by now they were right in the heart of the desert. A truly desolate place. She wished they had never come out today.

CHAPTER EIGHT

FOR the next two days Jo saw nothing of Bruce. He had taken the truck and was out prospecting in a desert area some distance from the house. Wistfully she had watched him leave, wishing she could ask to go with him but aware that when he was working he wanted no kind of distraction. Besides, there was plenty for her to do here. She divided her time between helping Sally prepare the guest houses and keeping Sandy amused.

This was in fact a way of giving her more instruction. Ross was also working some miles away with one of the rangers, relying on Brandy for transport, so Kari took the truck for two short sorties into the bush.

In his own quiet way he taught Jo as much as both Ross and Bruce had done. Because he was rather shy of her he addressed most of his comments to Sandy, who listened, fascinated; but Jo knew she too was supposed to listen and learn.

He stopped the truck several times when he thought something would be of interest to Sandy. Once he led them to the edge of a shallow pan where, half hidden by the pattern of thin undergrowth, it took sharp eyes to see the lacework of burrows in the hard dry soil. "There will be many, many mongoose there, young *Morena*," he said, "but they will be difficult to see unless we wait and watch. And we have no time. And over here," he moved stealthily forward, "is a place where the honey badger has been. He was seeking the wild honey."

"Can't we stay?" Sandy pleaded. "I've never seen a honey badger."

But Kari shook his head. "He is a shy animal, young *Morena*, he will be alone or perhaps with his mate. If he sees or smells you he will not appear, but come, there is an animal I can show you."

Again he walked along, in an easy, almost loping stride. He was rather broad for a Bushman, and, Ross had told her, had rather unusual features for a man of his race. The normally flat, slightly mongoloid features flared into high cheekbones and eyes full of expression. His tight black curls seemed to grow in an oddly triangular shape, giving an air of quiet humour. It was all these unusual characteristics, and his high degree of intelligence, that had made Uncle Harold pick him out.

Further round the pan he bent again and tapped at the hard sand. A pair of sharp eyes peered out at him and darted back again; then another pair, and another. Delighted, Sandy knelt down to get a closer look. "What are they, Kari? Not mongoose, I don't think."

"No, they are ground squirrels, many, many of them, and each generation stays in the same burrows. But this year," he squinted up at the clear sky, "I'm afraid they will be fewer. They are vegetarians, and with no water they will die." In a lower, sadder voice he added, "It will be a bad year for my people too."

As they climbed back into the truck Jo said, "Where are your people, Kari? Tell me about them."

"They come from deep in the Kalahari, lady, and I do not often see them. They are still very wild and do not understand why I have chosen to leave. But they are happy to see me. I do not belong to the Kalahari now, I belong to Nyala and the *Morena*." He gave a sideways glance at her. "*Morena* will make Nyala grow again . . . no one will take it from him."

"No, Kari," she said, watching the Bushman's face curiously, "no one will take it from him."

"Not the other *Morena*?"

She looked sharply at him. "Mr. Farley? Of course not." But she wondered why even the thought should have come into his mind.

On that day she learned to recognise the heart-shaped spoor of a waterbuck, the pugmark of a leopard; she learned that giraffe had passed by only an hour before and a small herd of buffalo had crossed their trail. A lone elephant had trampled a path through the bush and this seemed to worry Kari, the fact that the beast was alone. Every now and then when the truck was stopped he would bend close to the ground, perhaps run his fingers lightly across the sand and then, his ear cocked, listen. Like so many Bushmen he could hear sounds that no other human could, or perhaps it was not hearing, but a kind of instinct—that a sound was about to be heard.

Jo found she was already recognising the main animals on Nyala. Some, of course, were easy enough, but the many kinds of buck and larger antelope were easily confused. She now knew the small grey duiker by its quick movements and the two straight, sharp horns rising between its ears. Not too unlike them were the springbuck, but they seemed to move in larger herds. Now she could easily recognise the shy kudu with his proud head and white striped flanks, always hiding behind a group of trees, and the tiny steenbuck with its chestnut brown back and lighter chest. She was even beginning to know the kind of terrain in which to look for certain species, which animals needed more water than others and whether they could survive without grazing ground.

She and Sandy arrived back, tired but happy. Sandy, it was plain, could never have too much of the bush. He had an absolutely sure instinct with animals and an insatiable thirst for knowledge about them. Ten to one, Jo guessed, he would end up doing the same kind of job as Ross.

She showered and changed, tickled the waiting Goldie behind both ears, and collapsed in a canvas chair. Within seconds Saku had produced a long, cold fruit drink which she took gratefully, as Sally came in to join her.

"A message came through that the deep-freeze has arrived!" Sally informed her excitedly.

"So you'll be able to stock up with buffalo tails," Jo teased.

"For someone with a large appetite your stomach is very squeamish," her older sister retorted.

"I know. You really ought to learn to shoot, Sal, then you could control the whole thing yourself, from field to table as it were." She pulled a face at her sister.

"What's Bruce doing tomorrow?" Sally said suddenly.

"I don't know. Why?" Jo returned cautiously.

"Well, I could even give you a proper excuse for spending the day with him. We can get delivery of the deep-freeze as far as Nata. From there we're expected to pick it up at the local warehouse. And apparently it's not an awfully wise thing to leave goods lying around for too long."

"I'm sure Bruce would take me if he's back. He said he might be tonight. I'll walk down to his camp later."

"I thought that would make you sit up. You could also go into market there and get some cotton fabric for the guest rondavels. I've done all the measuring today." She paused. "Jo . . . I don't want you to bite my head off, or even accuse me of interfering, but have your feelings changed towards Bruce since you were in England?"

"Yes," replied Jo simply.

"You mean you no longer . . ."

"I mean nothing of the sort. My feelings are simply much stronger and surer. Bruce is the one person in the world for me."

"But . . ."

"No buts, Sal, because it won't make any difference to me—except perhaps to turn me against you. Oh, I know he has faults. I can even see that he wouldn't be an easy

121

man to live with, but that doesn't stop me falling in love with him."

"And he?" Sally said quietly.

Jo paused before she spoke. "I think he feels quite a lot for me. The year without news has drawn us together rather than widening the gap, but whether he's a marrying man, that's quite another matter. All I know is that for the moment I'm content to wait and see. The sort of life he lives isn't an easy one."

"He could change it," Sally pointed out.

"And blame me for the rest of his life? No, Sal, even you know that wouldn't be right. But I think I should tell you one thing . . ."

"Go on."

"If at the end of three months we have to leave Nyala, which I'm quite prepared for, although I'd do anything to stop it—I'm not going to come back to England."

"You . . . you mean you're going to stay here, in this country?"

"Not necessarily. I shouldn't think it would be possible to find much of a job here. No, I might go to South Africa or Kenya. I honestly don't know, Sal. I just feel I want to stay somewhere in Africa for a little longer. But," she added wryly, "I still wish we were able to keep Nyala."

Sally suddenly crossed the room and came to stand by her sister. "Look, Jo, I'm not going to try to persuade you one way or the other. You're twenty-one and you have to live your own life. But you're forgetting one important thing. If—and I know it's a very big if—we manage to make Nyala pay for itself there'll be no question of keeping it. We're going to sell it, remember, to help Alan. Not to do that would be a betrayal of all he's done for us, all he's given up for us. You do understand that, don't you, Jo?"

Jo nodded. "Of course I do." But in a way she had conveniently forgotten the real reason why she and Sally came out here. She had merely been indulging in a foolish little dream, thinking that one day Nyala could just conceivably be hers.

The two girls started dinner alone. Even Sandy had admitted defeat and gone to bed, hardly able to keep his eyes open. But Saku had just finished serving the soup when they heard Brandy clatter into the yard. A few minutes later Ross appeared at the door.

Both of them leapt to their feet, staring at him, shocked. His shirt was torn and streaked with blood. There were deep scratches down his face and he could have been rolling in dust.

"*Ross*!" Sally cried, "what on earth has happened? Saku," she called behind her, "bring a glass of brandy."

Ross tried to grin. "Not brandy, beer. I think I must have half the Kalahari desert down my throat."

Sally pulled away the shirt from his arm. The blood had dried into thick lines. "You can't leave that for a moment if you don't want to get infection. Where do you keep the antiseptic?"

But Saku was already there with both the beer and the bottle of antiseptic and a roll of cotton wool. Ross drained the glass at one gulp, then pushed the servant gently away. "Not until I've had a shower. I won't look quite such a sight then."

Jo found her voice at last. "What kind of animal did that to you?" she demanded.

"The most dangerous animal in the bush when you're on horseback," he replied, and disappeared into the bathroom.

Sally and Jo looked at each other soberly. "Funny," said Jo, "you see him walking all over the place, and Kari with Sandy and myself today, and you forget that some of the animals are dangerous."

"Well, he isn't afraid."

"Of course not. You couldn't last a minute in this job if you were afraid. Animals are supposed to scent fear, aren't they?"

They finished the soup, but Sally told Saku to hold the rest back until the *Morena* was ready. She then made sure there was a bowl of warm water, some bandages and plaster, which she set on a small table under the light.

Ross emerged still looking tired, but cleaner and fresher, the scratches on his face less raw and frightening. He saw Sally and shook his head.

"Just pass me the Dettol and a wad of cotton wool and I'll fix this in no time."

Sally merely said : "Sit down here and take off that shirt. Heaven knows what poison the animal infected you with. What was it anyway?" she said as she set to work on him.

His eyes crinkled into a rare smile. "No lions, no tigers, merely a very unpleasant brush with camel-thorn. That's what caused the scratches. I've always said there's more danger in the bush from thorn than pretty well any game."

He winced as Sally dabbed at the cuts on his face. "But why?" she demanded. "Were you simply not looking where you were going?"

"No, not quite that. I was caught napping by another buffalo and had to make a dash for it. I was in thorn country and Brandy simply took to his heels straight through the lot."

"Poachers again?" Jo said.

He turned to look at her. "Probably. I didn't get a chance to do too much investigation." He paused. "I'm sorry if I disappointed you by not getting attacked by a lion. I'm afraid it doesn't happen very often."

Jo flushed. Did he really think she wished that on him? But his humour was so dry she never could tell if he was laughing at her.

By the time Sally was finished with him the cuts looked less angry, but he seemed immensely tired.

Perhaps it had been a nearer scrape with the buffalo than he had told them.

He did not demur when Sally hustled him off to bed in just the way she had Sandy as soon as dinner was over. He told them he was worried about the continued decrease in the water supply, and the shorter the water became, so the problem of the poachers grew worse; they became more daring, more careless. From tomorrow, he said, he and Kari were going to have an all-out assault on them, getting up a rigorous system of patrols that would at least frighten off the worst of them.

Soon after he left them Sally announced that she too was going to bed. The heat had been particularly exhausting that day. Early nights were becoming necessary, for the hotter it became the earlier they all rose, to make the most of the freshest part of the day.

Jo was tired too, but she was determined to wait just a little longer for Bruce's return.

At last, when she was just beginning to nod off, she heard the crunch of wheels outside. She jerked awake and slipped out of the door to meet him, and as he climbed tiredly out of the truck it seemed the most natural thing in the world to run into his arms.

He was hot, dusty and sweaty, but the feel of those strong arms round her was immeasurably wonderful. And the kiss that seemed to tell her so much was even better. Then he pushed her away. "Hell, darling, I shouldn't be touching you in the state I'm in."

"I don't mind," she said happily. "I'm just glad to see you back. Go and have a shower and I'll make you some coffee. Anything to eat?"

"No, just coffee—and a can of beer if you can raise one."

She made the coffee herself in the silent kitchen, but thought he would probably prefer to drink it out at his own camp, so took the metal coffee pot down there and tried to stir the dead embers into some kind of life. It was surprising, how the temperature could drop so quickly at night.

She thought she might have tidied up for him, but the little camp site was immaculate. Here was a man who could pack up at short notice, a man all too obviously used to coping for himself, she thought wryly, and settled down to wait.

"Well," she said eagerly, as he finally appeared out of the darkness, "how did your first working day on Nyala go?"

"I must have met every tsetse fly in the bush," he answered, slapping himself liberally with lotion, "but otherwise the two days have acted as a preliminary survey. At least I've found the area in which to concentrate and have arranged to hire a couple of Africans to help with the first slog of prospecting. And it will be another two days before I get to the digging stage—especially as I shall have to go and pick up the boys some time tomorrow. Anyway, enough of me—what have you been doing these past two days?" He reached across and let a strand of her hair curl round his finger.

"Brushing up on my bush lore," she answered. "Kari has been giving lessons to Sandy and me. He probably knows almost as much as Ross does. I gather he was with my uncle for nearly ten years."

"And one day, without warning, he'll pack up and leave. They're all the same," Bruce said lazily.

"Not Kari," she answered. "Ross says he has the most incredible loyalty."

"Only while it suits him."

She frowned. "That doesn't sound like you, Bruce."

"Doesn't it? Then I must hide my cynicism more carefully. I've put my faith in the African just once too often. That's why I like to work alone as much as possible."

For some reason she felt uneasy at the turn the conversation was taking. She remembered what she wanted him to do tomorrow. Cautiously she brought up the subject of both the market and the deep-freeze. "But please, Bruce, say if you can't spare the time."

"Time? What's time?" he grinned. "If it means spending the day with you, then to market we'll go. I can pick up the boys on my way back. But it'll have to be a six o'clock start. Think you can manage it?"

"It's you, not me, that needs rest." She jumped up, letting go of his hand reluctantly. "Till six o'clock, then—and sleep well."

The truck was already waiting when Jo emerged sleepily into the fresh morning air. Bruce was leaning against the side throwing scraps of wood at Goldie who, surprisingly, was not in the mood for playing.

Bruce turned at the sound of her steps and Goldie relapsed into slumber once more. "Funny," he said, "I don't think she likes me."

"Impossible," Jo laughed. "Goldie loves everyone."

"Maybe," he shrugged, "but there must be exceptions to even a lion's love. I should have thought it really was time for her to go back into the bush."

"Well, Ross is trying, isn't he?"

"In a half-hearted sort of way. The only thing is to be ruthless—take her ten miles away, into a good hunting area, and dump her."

"But would she be able to hunt for herself?" Jo watched Goldie uncertainly.

"An animal is like a human. Throw it in the deep end and it will survive. The lion would go hungry for a couple of days and then by sheer force of circumstance have to fend for itself. Still, I'm a diamond man, not a zoologist, so I should learn to keep my mouth shut." He held out his hand to her. "Are you ready to go, Jo?"

"Yes, quite ready." She looked up happily into the sky. "It's going to be a wonderful day."

"Then don't let the others hear you say that. It won't be wonderful at Nyala until it rains."

Bruce drove in an easy relaxed way, talking most of the time, asking her questions, drawing her out about her early life and the background to Uncle Harold's unexpected legacy. She told him so much that she very nearly let slip about the whole purpose of coming to Nyala—a desperate attempt to raise money for Alan. But while she wanted to take him into her confidence, it was after all a family matter, and the fewer people who knew about the Frasers' plans, the better.

The route they took was the same as the one the two sisters had arrived at Nyala, across sandy, featureless desert, sprinkled only with scrub and thorn trees. There was hardly a movement in the hot still air and it seemed strange not to be looking for game.

They reached the small town mid-morning, after a stop for fruit and tea brewed by the side of the road. It took almost an hour to go through all the formalities of collecting the deep-freeze and arranging for it to be packed into the back of the truck. By then Jo was exhausted by the searing midday heat, so Bruce managed to arrange a cooling shower for her in the small restaurant where they were to have lunch. It was when she emerged, feeling fresher again, and drank a long, cold glass of fruit juice, that she discovered that there was a market place only a hundred yards down the road.

It was a large market, full of noise and colour, and at every stall where she paused to examine cloth they were immediately surrounded by the fiercest sales technique she had ever come across. But Bruce seemed to be able to cope, fending off the unwanted salesmen with dexterity, but whispering that she had better make up her mind soon or the prices would double.

Eventually she sifted through the dozens of rolls of material and chose the least violent colours, a different set for each of the guest-houses, as Sally had suggested. She only hoped Sally would approve of her choice. It was not exactly going to seem like the Ritz!

When they had taken the parcels back to the truck she then started to work her way through the other shopping list Sally had pressed into her hand, items from seeds to kitchen stores and fresh vegetables.

Of the latter there were plenty, piled up on the ground, tomatoes and avocadoes, potatoes and oranges and strange unrecognisable roots that Bruce told her were yams, the staple diet of the local Africans.

By the time that was finished Jo felt like a shower all over again, but instead it was time, Bruce said, to take her out to the best lunch the town had to offer.

They left in the early afternoon. Happy and replete and very drowsy, Jo dozed on the long journey home, her head nodding from side to side, until it finally came to rest against Bruce's shoulder.

She had no idea how long she had been asleep, but was awake with a sudden jerk as the truck slewed to a standstill. Bruce was shouting out of the window and a crowd of Africans were gesticulating and shouting back.

Jo felt she had woken in the middle of a dream, an unpleasant dream. "What is it, Bruce?" she said urgently. "Why are they shouting at us like that?"

"Because I've run over one of their wretched chickens. You'd think I'd killed their headman or something." He climbed out of the truck and continued the argument in the shade of one of the huts. Eventually he pulled some notes out of his pocket and slammed them on the flat surface of a fallen tree. As far as he was concerned that was the end of the affair and he turned his back on them all and climbed into the driver's seat.

Sheepishly two men slid out of the crowd, each carrying a bundle. Bruce jerked his head at them to get in the back, then without another glance swung the car round and drove off.

"Weren't they satisfied?" Jo said at last, when the worst of his anger had gone down.

"Apparently not. I apologised and offered the money

right from the beginning, but all they wanted was another live chicken. As if I could somehow conjure one out of thin air! I swear they're incapable of understanding anything but what they want to. A maddening race of people!"

Jo was wide awake by now and managed to stay so until the distant line of trees told them that Nyala was not far away. Today she was surprisingly glad to be home. And dusk was just about to fall.

As she climbed stiffly out of the truck Sandy ran to greet her.

"Did you have a good day, Jo? I've missed you today, really I have."

She gave the boy a hug. "I've missed you too, Sandy, but it's just as well you didn't come. There wasn't any game. And all Bruce and I did when we got there was the shopping."

"Oh well . . ." he pulled a face. "But before you do *anything* at all you must come and see Holly. I've been teaching her tricks. I want to see if she's forgotten them."

"Would after supper do?" Jo said hopefully.

"No, please, only for two minutes. It'll be dark later."

"All right, two minutes." And good-humouredly she allowed herself to be led across the grass.

She thought afterwards she must have stumbled, but over what she did not know. She was only aware of the slim dusky shape that reared up from the ground ahead of her and came at her like an arrow.

She screamed once as a shaft of pain shot through her leg and bent to clutch her ankle. Sandy turned and his quick eye saw the slim shape shoot off towards the river. Without a second's hesitation he yelled: *"Mamba!"*

"Oh, God, no! Bruce," she called faintly. But he was already there, fumbling at her trouser-clad leg.

Sandy was still shouting. "You're wasting time. You want a knife, I know you do!" and when Bruce remained with her, rocking her gently in his arms, he raced for the house.

The next few seconds were a blur. She was aware only of Ross looming up behind her, pushing Bruce out of the way without ceremony. There was a short angry exchange between the two men before she felt some rope or string tightened round her thigh, then the awful pain of a knife shearing without mercy into her leg. Before she could cry out, she fainted.

CHAPTER NINE

THERE was a thick, damp steaming forest and yet she was trying to push her way through it to find water. She knew that if she did not find water soon her throat would dry up completely. On and on she seemed to be travelling and getting no nearer her destination. She would not give in, and yet she knew she would have to unless she found water. The trees dripped all about her, but when she held out her hand to catch the drips there was only the crackle of dryness.

Suddenly, miraculously, the forest was gone and ahead was a sheet of shining, shimmering water. Or was it a mirage? She started to run, but her feet were leaden and there was a terrible pain in her leg. Only a few yards to go and finally she reached out to the blessed coolness of the water. As she touched it, it disappeared and she cried out at last.

Very close to Jo there was a voice that sounded exactly like her sister's. "I think she's coming to," Sally was saying.

Coming to where? Jo thought foolishly, and as she opened her eyes the nightmare was gone.

"Could I have some water?" she said clearly. At least that part of it was true; her throat felt drier than sand.

She drank long and deeply and looked at Sally properly. "Why are you looking so worried?"

"I ... we ... were all worried about you. Snakebite can be a killer around here, apparently."

Snakebite ... of course, that was the dull throb in her leg. But what had actually happened was a bit hazy except that she remembered Bruce holding her tightly in his arms.

"Is . . . is it all right? My leg, I mean."

Sally nodded. "Ross acted like lightning. He was pumping the serum into your leg almost before I realised what had happened . . ." She turned as there was a tap at the door. "Oh, Ross, she seems fine, thank goodness."

He hovered in the doorway. Whatever he might have been feeling was masked by a frown. "You had us worried for a moment when young Sandy called out 'mamba'. You've him to thank as much as anyone for swift action—and the fact he knows his snakes."

"A mamba? That's one of the dangerous ones, isn't it?"

"Just about the most deadly in these parts," he told her. "We don't see the black variety, only the green, and to be perfectly honest not many of those. I'm not entirely sure it *was* a green mamba that bit you, because you've been so lightly affected. Wearing trousers helped, of course, so there was only one puncture, but even so the venom is so strong that it would have laid you out for much longer than this." He turned to Sally. "I think that leg will need fresh dressings. Can you manage it, or do you want me to do it?"

"I'll be all right now," Sally told him, "but I'll call if I'm in any doubt."

He turned to leave and Jo pulled herself higher on to the pillows. "Ross . . ."

He turned in the doorway.

"Thank you."

"All in a day's work. Elephants, lions—humans!" But there was no malice in his voice.

As Sally bandaged her leg, Jo said, "How did he know what to do?"

"I gather coping with snakebite is one of the first things you have to learn round here. He applied a tourniquet, cut open your leg at the puncture and got most of the poison out that way before injecting the serum. When I asked him later he told me that he had taken a first aid course and he keeps a fair number of basic medicines here. Don't forget the whole of Nyala relies on him. The nearest doctor is about a hundred miles."

A little later Saku brought in a tray of food. Jo was surprised to find it breakfast time. Apparently Ross had also insisted on giving her a sleeping draught to work off the worst of the pain. The African bowed ceremoniously and hoped the lady was feeling better. The *Morena* was a very clever man, was he not?

"Very clever," Jo agreed gravely.

When he had gone and Jo was drinking her coffee she looked towards her sister and said, "Sally, where's Bruce?"

For a moment Sally looked uncomfortable. "He's waiting for Ross to leave the house, then he's coming to see you."

"Waiting for Ross to leave? Why? What on earth are you talking about?"

Sally sighed. "Look, in a moment I've got to go and fetch him. He'll tell you his side of the story and I honestly don't know the rights and wrongs of it, because I was only on the scene as Ross was dealing with your leg. All I know is that the two of them had a dreadful row."

A chill settled on Jo. "You mean over me?"

"Yes, at least over the snakebite. All I ask, Jo, is for you not to take sides. You were unconscious so can't possibly know which of them did the right thing. The only important thing is that you are all right. Personally, I'm glad Ross took no chances. There isn't time to wait and wonder about a snakebite."

Jo pushed her hair back from her face and when she spoke her voice was dangerously quiet. "Well, you haven't told me what the row was about, but you have told me whose side you were on. I think I'd like to see Bruce. Now."

Sally shrugged. She knew when there was no point at all in talking to Jo, so she got up from her chair, straightened out the bed and went in search of Bruce.

Five minutes later his tall figure was blocking the doorway.

"Hello, Bruce," she said softly.

He paused just for a moment, then he was beside her and she was in his arms, so tightly that she thought he would squeeze the breath from her.

"Oh, God, Jo, I thought I'd lost you!"

"I'm afraid you don't get rid of me quite as easily as that." She tried to speak lightly, but her voice came out all choky.

He held her away from him. "You are all right, aren't you?"

"Of course. I've got a bit of a headache and my leg aches, but beyond that there's nothing wrong with me. I gather I had a lucky escape. It's Sally, funnily enough, who hates snakes. Ross said..."

The name slipped out without her thinking. She had not wanted to start anything, but it acted like a red rag to a bull.

His fists closed and unclosed. "Andrews? What I'd like to say about that man could not be said in fit company. It's no thanks to him that you had a lucky escape. He'd have had half your leg off if I hadn't been around."

"What...what did happen, Bruce?"

He slumped on the end of the bed. "Oh, you were bitten all right, but not by a mamba. At the time Andrews was more eager to take the boy's word than mine. Sandy yelled 'Mamba' and that was the signal for Andrews to go in for amateur surgery. When I tried to tell him, all I got was rough enough handling to knock me off my feet."

"Oh, Bruce, I am sorry. But if it had been a mamba . . ."

"*If*. But it wasn't."

"I suppose he could have thought it was not worth taking any chances."

"He could have done anything. What he actually did included accusing me afterwards of panicking, of acting like a raw recruit in the bush and finally of trying to kill you instead of saving your life."

"Oh, Bruce, no!" Now she was truly appalled.

"Oh, yes," he answered bitterly. "I could probably have taken it if this hadn't all been flung at me after the great Doctor Andrews had pronounced you out of danger. I can't honestly see us sitting down at the same dinner table after this, Jo."

She was miserably aware that Bruce believed he had come to a point of no return and while she had genuinely tried to do what Sally said—not take sides, her sympathy was now swinging towards him. Anything could have been done and said in the heat of the moment—the emergency, if Ross had genuinely believed there to have been one—but to say those things, to accuse another man without justification, simply because he had taken a different point of view, was surely unforgivable.

While she was trying to think of what to say to Bruce, there was a single tap at the door and Sandy's head appeared round it. But, extraordinarily, his grin of delight at seeing her sitting up, none the worse for her experience, changed to a scowl as he saw Bruce. In an extra polite voice he said, "I'm glad to see you're all right, Jo. I'll come and visit you properly later. When you're alone." The door closed with a little snap.

"What was all that about?" she asked.

He sighed. "Young Sandy is a faithful follower. Your Mr. Andrews can do no wrong, but I dared to disagree with him, so am cast as a villain of the piece."

"But that's ridiculous," Jo protested. "Just wait until I've had a word with him."

"And tried to influence him? I think the whole subject is better left, darling. Even a nine-year-old can say rather smugly, 'But you were unconscious, what do you know about it?' No, forget it, Jo; the main thing is that you're all right. My only comment is to keep an even warier eye on Andrews. A man who can be so brutal could provide all sorts of problems."

Sally forced Jo to stay in bed for the rest of that day and although Jo grumbled she found that she must have been tired and so slept on and off most of the time. By the time she got up the ache in her leg had eased considerably, but again Sally persuaded her to take it easy and produced the first of the guest curtains for her to sew. There was no sign of Bruce, but he had left her a note saying he was going off again for a couple of days, to start some of the more advanced prospecting work with the two Africans.

As she sewed, Sandy came and sat beside her.

"Did you know Dad's coming back tomorrow? He's going to stay the whole weekend and we're all going croc-hunting."

"You may be going croc-hunting, but not me," she shuddered.

"Oh, Sally says you'll be quite well enough. I asked her, honestly. And Ross says you can come."

"And what if I don't want to?"

"But you must," he said in tones of disbelief. "Everyone wants to hunt their first croc."

She laughed, unable to admit to her disgust. Still, if it was part of Nyala life, it might be prudent to say at least she had *seen* a crocodile hunt.

Bored with sitting about, Sandy announced that he was going to take Holly for a walk. "She'll follow me nearly as well as she'll follow you," he said proudly. "I wish she could come back home with me."

"I know how you feel, Sandy. Just as I wish we could keep her as a pet, but soon she'll have to go back into the bush, just like Goldie, I suppose."

"I know it really," he said. "Ross has explained it all to me. Do you know, Jo, he knows simply everything about animals. Not like . . ." he stopped himself abruptly, but could not help adding, "It *was* a mamba, you know, that beautiful pale green colour. If it had only been *him* there, you'd be dead."

Jo winced at his outspokenness. "Look, Sandy, I'm all right, and that's all that matters. I think we should all forget what happened, and honestly we'll never really be able to say for certain whether it was a mamba or not."

"But you didn't hear what he said to Ross . . ."

"*Sandy*!" That was Ross standing in the doorway, looking unbelievably stern.

Mustering his remaining dignity, Sandy jumped up, saying quickly, "I said I was going to take Holly for a walk. I think I'll go now."

Jo watched the small upright figure disappear. "He's very loyal, Ross."

"Too loyal, I'm afraid. If you put that much trust in a person at some time or another you're bound to be disappointed. Still, if Sandy turns out anything like his father, he'll be all right. By the way, Neil will be here tomorrow. I expect you're wondering if he has any news about Nyala safaris."

"Yes. Although . . ."

He came and sat on the chair opposite her, his eyes narrowed and keen. She wished suddenly she knew more about Ross Andrews, what made him tick. Sometimes he was quite talkative, but never about himself. In a strange sort of way she knew no more about him than on the first day they arrived at Nyala. It was as though he did not want to get close to anyone, even a child like Sandy. Was he afraid they would let him down, or that he would let them down? Or had he something to hide?

"Although what?" he was saying. "Have you changed your mind about the safaris here?"

"Oh, no," she shook her head vehemently. "It's the only way to make the place pay, I'm convinced of that. But I realise more every day how dependent we are on you."

"And you think I might let you down. Those thoughts don't sound like yours, Jo. Has Bruce Farley been talking to you?"

"No, but now you come to mention it..."

"Look," he stood up abruptly and she saw the shut-down expression come over his face, "if you're going to bring up your snakebite, then I think it would be better if I left you now."

"That's unfair," she protested, "if you won't even listen."

"You mean I should listen to you telling me Farley's point of view? No, Jo, I did what was right, and if the same thing happened again that's just what I would do. With snakes there's no time to stop and think and discuss."

"That wasn't what I meant," she said tightly. "You know I'm grateful for what you did for me. But that you should attack Bruce simply for holding his point of view..."

"I see, so that's what he told you. It's not important to me, Jo. All I know is that he's your friend, perhaps even something more, if I'm not mistaken, therefore you have a right to have him here. But as far as the running of this reserve goes—and that covers quite a lot of things—then what I say goes. Perhaps you'd better let him know that, because though you may not think it, I'm a peace-loving man, but I don't like to be told how to do the job I'm paid for."

"Bruce has also spent his life in Africa," she flung at

him, stung because he seemed to think he was always right. "Are you as arrogant as to think no one can tell you anything?"

But he had had enough. He glanced at his watch. "I think I've wasted enough time. I just wanted to say that I'm glad to see you up and about. If there's anything you want, just let me know."

"I hope I won't have to."

"I realise that, but the offer still stands. You could tell Farley when he returns that I hope he won't take his anger out on Neil. We'll look forward to him dining with us—and crocodile-hunting if he feels like it." He turned on his heel and left her.

She picked up a magazine, then flung it down angrily. Oh, what was the use with a man like that!

As dusk fell the following evening they heard the sound of Neil Brand's truck long before it came into sight. After an earlier show of nonchalance Sandy was suddenly excited to see his father. He tugged at Sally's hand. "Come with me and meet him, I've got so much to tell him."

"Then you won't want me," she laughed, but she allowed herself to be led.

Ross, leaning over the verandah rail smoking his pipe, turned to Jo and said idly, "Has Sally got any strong ties in England?"

"Someone special, you mean?"

He nodded.

"No," Jo answered, "there's no one special." She looked at him shrewdly. "Why do you ask?"

"She would make someone a wonderful wife," he mused.

She turned quickly away, struggling with the small flare of jealousy. Neil, now Ross. Could Sally never do any wrong?

She led the way down into the garden as Sandy and his father came towards the house, chattering nineteen to the dozen. Sally walked alongside them adding her comments when asked for.

"Well, it all sounds great," Neil put his hand on his son's shoulder, "but you mean to tell me that no one has got eaten by a lion?"

He was rewarded by a withering glance that abruptly changed to one of triumph. "No, but Jo got bitten by a snake—a green mamba!"

Neil glanced at the bandage on Jo's leg as he shook hands with her. "Well, you've got scars to prove it, by the look of things. Exaggeration or truth from my son?"

"It was a snake all right," she laughed, "but there seems some doubt about the identification. Anyway, Ross dealt with it very swiftly."

"Yes, he would," Neil said calmly, and turned to his friend. "Oddly enough I was going to ask you last time how you were off for serum."

They all continued companionably into the house, and while Neil showered, Ross poured them all drinks. So Bruce was not coming tonight, Jo thought with a pang of disappointment. She wanted him beside her so much. And yet in another way she was less certain of being able to cope with icy politeness between the two men. Perhaps tomorrow was better after all. Another day to cool down and perhaps she would be able to talk to him first. At least Neil would be a calming influence.

Once again Sally had produced a magnificent dinner, organising it without fuss, but she pinked with delight at all the compliments.

"We must have guests more often," Ross winked at his friend, as he raised his glass to Sally. "It gets away from the interminable warthog—or buffalo tail!" That last was aimed at Jo, but tonight she was able to laugh with the others.

"Talking of guests," Neil sat back in his chair, happy and replete, "I've had a couple of talks with my brother about your safari idea. He's over-enthusiastic if anything, so I thought I'd better play down Nyala's amenities. He says he could produce six people tomorrow, but can't you take more? I told him no quite firmly—at least until you had got into your stride, but he seems to think this operation could be run something like a private grouse shoot in England. The individuality of the thing being the keynote—living *en famille*, etc. Anyway, I told him I was only the go-between and had no idea how near you were to starting the thing, so he had a proposal to make. As soon as you even think you can cope with say four guests, he'll come down himself with three guinea-pigs. You will treat them exactly as you would any strangers and at the end of the week he—and they—can tell you where you're going right or wrong, give any suggestions about the future and of course about costing. They'll pay their way, naturally, but you did say you had no idea what to charge people. Well, that's his province. Now, what do you say to that?"

Sally looked across at Ross. "I feel a bit overwhelmed. When do you think we would be ready?"

He smiled wryly. "Never, if it were left to me. When do you think you could have two guest-houses ready?"

Sally looked thoughtful. "Well, if Jo and I sew hard, and that now is really all there is, less than a week. But that's only the beginning."

"I know. But say another week to plan supplies of food and make sure the place is in working order, then we could certainly cope with four guinea-pigs—if that's what they really regard themselves as."

"A fortnight, then," Neil nodded complacently. "I'll radio him first thing on Monday when I get back."

Jo and Sally's eyes met in faint panic. They were now being rushed, when before it had been the other way round. "Do you really think we can manage it?" Jo said faintly.

"You'll have to," Ross pointed out. "Your three months are slipping away. Besides, let's get a test case over. Neil's brother might see all kinds of difficulties that we can't possibly cope with. Then we would have to do a huge rethink."

So the matter seemed to be settled, and once again Jo marvelled at the way Ross had coaxed Sally to do what he wanted almost without her realising. She did not know whether she was pleased or irritated. But she did suddenly think that the prospects of holding on to Nyala were not quite so gloomy after all.

As they sat drinking coffee afterwards Neil looked at them all and, with a glint in his eye, challenged them: "Who's game for crocodile-hunting tonight?"

The girls said nothing. Ross, of course, took up the challenge. "Well, tonight's good enough for a start, since you've only got tomorrow with us. We could get the feel of the river at least."

Sandy rushed across to his father. "You are going to let me come, aren't you?"

"On two conditions. One, that you go to bed immediately so that you get a couple of hours' sleep, and second, that when we're out you do exactly what you're told, without a single question. If you fail in that, there'll be a three-year wait for the next go."

Sandy nodded and without a word disappeared to his room.

Ross checked the time and said, "Well, I've a couple of things to do first. Look after the girls, Neil, for half an hour, then we'll go out and check the equipment and the boat."

"Aren't you afraid for Sandy?" Jo said curiously. "I know he's marvellously adaptable, but *crocodiles* . . ."

Neil smiled. "I'm not afraid for him, because I trust him. Even so I wouldn't take him yet to somewhere like Okavango, where it's all done by boats and in the right areas there are more crocs than humans. No, tonight isn't a real hunt. To start with I guarantee there are only two adult beasts and they must be in a fairly limited stretch of the river. I'll be the only one in a boat; the rest of you—if you two are coming—will be on land. I'm afraid you could hardly call this the real thing, but it's a good enough start for amateurs."

Jo was still deciding whether she would join the hunting party and try to rid herself of a fear of crocodiles when she heard Sally say : "Neil, now we both have you on our own for a moment, there's something we wanted to ask you."

"Go ahead, it sounds very mysterious."

"It's about Uncle Harold. You see, we know so little about him. But last year, he did ask you to look us up without giving away your connection with him, didn't he?"

He hesitated only a second. "I'm afraid he did. I hope you don't think it was too underhand. At the time, I did as he asked; there seemed no harm in it."

"No, it doesn't matter at all," Sally said, "but it would be interesting to know why, and even more important, why Jo was left out of the will when you must surely have reported that there were three of us. It doesn't matter anyway, because what's Alan's and mine is Jo's too, but we felt there had to be a reason."

"To answer all that properly would be to know and understand your uncle. I knew him and I liked him, but I never really understood him. Deep down he was an unhappy man. He had never talked of his family in England until he heard that I was going and then he gave me this commission to find out all I could about you. It seemed terribly important to him that I should think a lot of you so that in turn he could have the right image of you all. I think he wanted to feel you could do things for yourselves, just like he did. Hence possibly the odd will concerning Nyala.

"But as far as Jo is concerned, one of the last things he

said to me was before I left: 'Find out if there's a third child. After all these years I must know'. Of course I came back and told him that Jo was very much alive and kicking. And that's another funny thing, Jo, I also told him that I would have known you were his niece anywhere. Same colouring, even the same rather forthright nose, if you'll forgive me. I suppose you take after your father."

"No," said Jo flatly, "I was always the odd man out in the family, nothing like either my father or mother."

A sudden silence fell and they must all have been thinking the same thing. Jo was thinking of all those books about Africa in the trunk in the attic.

Neil said gently, "I'm a clumsy great fool, aren't I? Now I've filled both your minds with the kind of doubts that we can never answer. I'm sorry, I'm truly sorry."

"It's all right." Jo got up quickly. "I'll be back in a minute, just want to get my croc-hunting gear together," she finished with an attempt at lightness.

She went to her room and leaned out of the window into the cool of the night. So the mystery was solved—or was it? She thought of her parents and how happy they had been together before they died, and even the special place, as youngest of the family, she had had in her father's heart. Those facts she was quite, quite sure of. So whatever had happened in the past had no influence on her present life, only the fact that she was here, at Nyala now.

It was foolish to be so suddenly moved near to tears. More than anything now she wished she had met her uncle—just once. But wishing was only for children, so she dashed her face in cold water and dried it thoroughly, then turned to go back.

No, she didn't feel sociable now.

She sat in the darkness feeling suddenly lonely, wishing that Bruce was here. Was she really the outsider she felt herself to be at the moment?

In a pool of light from the house she saw Ross walk across the yard. He hesitated a moment as though he sensed he were being watched. He was alone and did not seem to mind. But his life was dependent on none. In some strange way that provoked her. One day she would show Ross Andrews she was not the wilful child he thought she was. One day she would be able to take him down a peg or two.

CHAPTER TEN

FROM ten to ten-thirty the household seemed to be in a whirl of activity and both girls wisely kept out of the way, except when asked to do a specific job. When everything was ready they were told to waken Sandy.

All were wearing long trousers and boots when they met outside the house for final instructions. Kari and two other Africans were also there to lend a hand.

First of all Neil examined the sky. Fortunately it was a dark, moonless night, the only real possibility for successful hunting. Ross had marked the crocodiles down to a particular stretch of the river and that had been sectioned off with weighted netting into two halves. They would do one tonight and the other tomorrow.

In the boat was Neil, gun at the ready, with Kari acting as both steersman and oarsman. They would start to move silently down river, in complete darkness, to give as little warning as possible, hoping to pick up the gimlet glare of those ruby red eyes. Ross and the other boys would move down the bank, always ahead of the boat, hoping for a chance shot. Otherwise they had ropes at the ready to haul their captive ashore, and also an axe for that all-important final blow across the spine.

Jo was not exactly looking forward to the event, but she could not be left out now and, besides, a feeling of tense excitement was being generated through them all. Even the Africans, used to a surfeit of game, were aware that a crocodile kill was unusual at Nyala.

For the first hour nothing much happened, as Kari rowed steadily downstream, slowly, going from bank to bank whenever the river broadened.

Suddenly there was a subtle tightening of the

atmosphere, and although nothing had actually changed, they were all still, waiting. Even the quiet dip of the oars had ceased.

Jo strained her eyes, staring at the dim outline of the boat, and the space just ahead of it. As the lamp at the prow, where Neil was sitting, gun poised, was switched on, she caught a glimpse of the two jutting red eyes, glowing, just a few inches apart. As the monster became aware of the boat, it rose slightly, ready to submerge, and at that second Neil fired.

He hit it all right, Jo saw that, but it was not to be the end of this particular crocodile. She had heard stories of the horror of thrashing tails and the great horny bodies manoeuvring to tip up the marauding boat, but somehow, seeing this great beast in action was much more horrifying than mere imagination. The spray from its lashing tail drenched them all, but all the men stayed exactly at their posts, waiting for the moment to kill.

Sally clutched at Jo. "It looks terribly dangerous. Nothing would ever get me in one of those boats!"

Jo felt too afraid for Neil and Kari even to answer. The light from the prow of the boat, now switched on like a miniature searchlight, picked out the scene like something from a science fiction film.

Suddenly the monstrous head reared high above the water, there was a single shot and as it started to sink the men on the bank threw the rope and hooks. A few minutes later it lay on the bank. Cautiously both Sally and Jo approached and looked down. Most animals, however wild, looked peaceful, almost harmless, in death; but not the crocodile. The rows of vicious teeth were still locked in a snarl.

Neil had landed the boat and come to examine his catch. "Not a large one, I'm afraid, but female. The point is, has she any young round here?"

"Or a mate," put in Ross.

"If he's around, then we'll find him tomorrow, but if by

any chance we don't—well, he won't stay round here for long, a single lone croc."

Sandy was bending down, fingering the horny skin with interest. "What's it worth, Dad?"

"A lady's small handbag, I daresay, you mercenary young scamp. Now, off to bed with you, pronto!"

Sandy's face fell and as he backed away added, "You're not going to skin it tonight, are you?"

"No, we're not. It's much too late. Don't worry, I won't let you miss anything."

Sally was still looking taken aback when Neil said to her with a smile: "I'm afraid he's still going through the ghoulish stage."

Sally shuddered. "I envy him. I wish I had such a strong stomach."

"It's something you'll get if you stay out here long enough."

He gave orders for the crocodile to be left immersed in water until the morning, then he would supervise the skinning operation. Both Jo and Sally turned thankfully away.

Ross was relieved that at least one crocodile had been found. "You've earned a celebration drink, Neil, doing my dirty work for me."

Neil shook his head. "You should know by now it's not work to me, but pleasure. It's good to get my eye in before going up to Okavango."

As they walked back to the house Jo said curiously, "What's it like up there, and how many crocs do you get in a night?"

"On a good night maybe six or seven. It depends how lucky I am, or how energetic, and how many men I take with me. As to the country, it's difficult to describe. On the edge of the swampland is a broad river, crystal clear and wonderful to drink. You can see pike and bream and incredible shoals of sardines. And on its banks are some of the most beautiful butterflies in the world, painted in every brilliant colour you can think of. And of course there are the birds, blue rollers, bee-eaters, and sacred ibis, again in every imaginable colour."

"It sounds like paradise."

"It is, but even paradise has its serpents, mosquito and tsetse fly and the dangers of malaria and sleeping sickness. And," he added dryly, "you have to watch out for rabies!"

They had moved into the sitting room and Saku produced nightcaps for them all. Jo discovered she was very wide awake and persuaded Neil to go on talking.

"Well," he continued, "you have to get used to the smell of croc—you had a slight whiff of it tonight—then you go inland, into the real swamps. Sometimes the river is only a few feet wide, sometimes there are broad lagoons. Everywhere the vegetation is thick, tall reeds stretching endlessly along the banks, with papyrus and every kind of tree you can think of. The land is dangerous; you're never quite sure whether you are stepping on to terra firma, or merely an island, looking safe enough, but in reality composed of a raffia-like substance, all the entangled roots of the reeds.

"The swamplands have a kind of beauty all of their own. You either love it or long to escape from it. It is certainly another world. And the game ... well, apart from the crocodiles, you'll find plenty of hippo ... and very tetchy they can be ... as well as leopard and elephant and most of the usual kinds. You've also got to get used to even more mosquitoes, tsetse fly and particularly nasty leeches." He looked across at the two girls, listening enthralled. "Well, have I put you off for life, or do you want to come on my next trip?"

Both laughed and Jo said stoutly, "Well, give me another few months, until I've overcome all the problems of Nyala, then I'd be game. But I don't think I could ever get really used to the crocodiles. One is bad enough, but seeing them in quantity ..." She shivered.

As they finally got up, stretching, agreeing that it had been a wonderful evening, the headlights of a truck pierced the darkness outside. Jo's heart leapt. Bruce was home!

Neil knowing nothing of the tensions between Bruce and Ross, said, "What a pity. Bruce looks as if he's arrived just an hour too late. Still, let's hope we have the same luck tomorrow night."

Jo doubted whether Bruce would come up to the house that evening, but he had apparently run short of water and arrived only a few minutes later, carrying an empty drum.

Neil hailed him. "I was just saying you'd missed all the excitement. Crocodile excitement. How have you been doing out in the prospecting field?"

"Too early to say. There are both good signs and bad signs. I'm a poor speculator. Anyway, good to see you again, Neil." He smiled at Sally and came directly across to Jo and kissed her.

She felt rather than saw Ross's disapproval. That made her response more eager. There was something very final about a public kiss, almost like an announcement. She put aside the thought that with all the difficulties that lay ahead still, it might have been better for their relationship to remain a private thing.

He let his arms rest possessively across her shoulders. "How's the leg, darling?"

"But better. I only notice it if I'm standing for some time. There was so much going on this evening down by the river I didn't even give it a thought. Neil caught a vicious-looking crocodile. You'll have to come and look at it in the morning." She found herself speaking quickly, as if suddenly to cover up his intimacy towards her.

Ross said abruptly, "For me, it's time for bed. Thanks again, Neil, I'll see you in the morning."

"Did you remember to lock up Holly?" Jo asked

him. She had made herself responsible for this before the snakebite, but had forgotten for a couple of days.

"Of course. She's as safe as houses. But you do realise it will soon be time to let her join her own kind?" He was watching her with that cool, unnerving gaze.

"Naturally," she retorted, "but not just yet. She's still only a baby."

"Even babies have to grow up," was his parting shot.

Once again Jo went to bed angry with Ross. He still took pleasure in rubbing her up the wrong way. She would have liked to go out to Bruce when he took the water back, but as she made the move, Sally's hand was like steel on her arm.

Outside their bedrooms, Jo shook her off. "You're not my guardian, you know, only a sister."

"Even a sister can tell you two not to make such a public display . . . I know, I know," she added tiredly, when Jo started to protest, "it's not my business to stop you falling in love or making a fool of yourself. But you know perfectly well how difficult things are here and with a potentially explosive situation between Ross and Bruce, heaven knows what could happen. Just at this very moment we need a happy working team if we're going to put on a show for this first safari, not friction and bad temper."

"You've made yourself perfectly clear," Jo said coldly. "Now, do you mind if I go to bed?" She closed the door behind her with a snap.

Jo was awoken by an odd noise outside her window. At first she thought it was a bird, until she realised it was some kind of tapping noise on her window. She glanced at her watch. It was not six o'clock.

She threw a housecoat round her shoulders and crossed to the window. Bruce was outside clad only in a pair of shorts. He put a finger to his lips and beckoned to her to come out and down to his camp. She nodded and did not stop to do more than comb her hair and slip on shorts and a shirt.

The coffee pot was already heating on his small fire. He looked up at the sound of her steps. "I couldn't sleep, so I decided to wake you up to share my wakefulness with me. Did you mind?"

"Did I mind? Don't be silly." She took the hand held out to her and sat down beside him. "I . . . I would have come down last night, but I didn't think it was a very politic move."

"Don't tell me Jo, that you care what people think."

"Of course not." Her denial was immediate. "At this moment I care about you very much, but I also care about Nyala. *You* want it to be a success as much as I do."

"Naturally. Come here, I can't have you looking as worried as that."

When he let her go, she was breathless, wondering why she was even faintly worried at him kissing her last night. Let them all see. Let them all know. She was proud of their feelings for each other. But somehow she must try to keep the peace.

"Bruce," she began, "I've got a favour to ask you."

His eyes half closed and he smiled lazily. "I know, be friends with your Mr. Andrews."

"He's not my Mr. Andrews, and I don't want you to be friends with him, just to rub along with him until things are settled one way or another."

"Why not ask him?"

"I will if you want me to, but I hardly know him, at least not in such a personal way."

"Aren't you being a little naïve, Jo?"

"Naïve?" She was puzzled. "I don't know what you mean."

"No, I don't believe you do. You may not know him in what you call a personal way, but he would certainly like to know you a little better."

She stared at him. "You must be mad! He thinks I'm

some kind of nincompoop he's got to put up with for three months. He hardly ever tries to make the best of it, except when he's being patronising."

"Then you haven't seen the way he looks at you. Why do you think I marched in and kissed you like that last night? Not just to embarrass you, Jo, I promise you. No, to show them what I felt about you. To stake my claim, if you like. Even your sister has been influenced by Andrews. The next thing we'll hear is that Neil Brand is joining in the general disapproval."

"Oh, Bruce, I don't know what to say. You're wrong about Ross, I know you are. It all stems from my wretched snakebite."

"No. No, not really, although it didn't help. I'm afraid my opinion of him isn't as high as yours. I think he probably knows a fair amount about game, but I don't think he runs this place half as competently as you think he does. I suppose you've thought what he would gain if he could persuade you over on to his side."

"His side? But I'm not on anyone's side," she cried. "Only Nyala's. I love it here; I really do. To me Ross Andrews is just part of the place like Kari, or Saku ... or even Goldie," she said helplessly. "You can't really be jealous, Bruce."

"I am. I'm jealous of any man who looks at you like he does. Covetous is the word. Ross Andrews is out to feather his nest, nothing more. And that's the reason I don't trust him with you, or Nyala."

Jo did not know what to say. She always knew that loving Bruce was not going to be easy, but that he should feel so strongly about Ross Andrews was ridiculous. Somehow she had to convince him that Ross was merely doing the job he was being paid for. With absolute certainty she knew his opinion of her. Not very high. And it really didn't matter except ... except there was something disconcerting about that cool, calculating gaze he sometimes turned on her.

Suddenly there was a noise from the house. It sounded like Sandy shouting. And then the calling became shrill: "Ross, Ross . . . Dad! Please come quickly!"

Jo jumped up, startled. "Something's wrong, Bruce, we must go." She let go of his hand and started to run across the patch of land from the river.

The commotion came from the back of the house. There she found Sandy, sobbing wildly, clinging to his father. Beside them Ross stood, watching the swinging door of Holly's empty cage, his eyes empty of emotion.

Jo looked from one man to another. "Where is she?"

"The door was open like this," Ross said bluntly. "Someone must have come after I did last night."

Jo's heart sank. She knew what little chance a trusting young animal like Holly would have in Nyala. "Have you looked for her?" she demanded.

"Not yet."

"Well, let's start." And when Ross hesitated she added savagely, jerking her head towards Sandy, "Well, it's worth doing something, isn't it?"

It was Ross who found Holly's remains, not three hundred yards from the house. When he told Sandy, quite directly, yet with great gentleness, the boy did not flinch. The bush was a hard school in which to learn. And after all, his crying had already been done.

But Jo was near to tears, remembering the gentle brown eyes, the delicate movements, the gradual building up absolute trust. One of the worst things in the world, she decided, was to have one's faith shattered.

When Sandy went off with his father and Saku told them that breakfast was ready, Jo turned to Ross. "No one would have deliberately opened the door, it's just not possible. I suppose checking to see that it was closed was too lowly a job for you after all. If you'd only asked me last night, or Sally . . ."

"You judge people harshly, don't you? Your standards for others are not very high. But of course, I forget, I'm the sort of man who sets lions on visitors, so it would be quite in keeping to throw a mere fawn to the predators."

"Now you're being sarcastic," she returned, perilously near to tears. "Why can't you ever face the truth?"

"Because I happen to be a man who feels very strongly about the truth." Now his face was black and thunderous. Only five minutes ago it had been full of gentleness when he talked to Sandy. "I may have many, many faults, but telling lies is not one of them. Before you accuse so wildly just look into the purity of your own motives. You've got to grow up, Jo. I don't think we shall get Nyala successfully on its feet as long as your friend Farley is here."

"That's exactly what he said about you!" she hurled back at him.

She hadn't meant to say that, because she was now doing exactly what she had begged Bruce not to—raise the already sizzling temperature at Nyala.

They were still standing facing each other, perhaps both wishing they could retract the hurtful words, when Sally came out. She quickly took in the strained atmosphere, but it was to Ross she turned.

"I think," she said, "there's a message coming through to you on the radio telephone."

"Thank you, Sally," he said politely, and as he turned to go he paused. "Oh, by the way, your sister really does think that Bruce Farley can do my job better than I can. Perhaps you would talk things over with her and decide once and for all whether you want me to stay or not. It's *your* decision, Sally. There's only room for one warden at Nyala."

Sally watched him go, then looked her younger sister up and down. "Well, you really are determined to muck things up, aren't you? Why," she sighed, "do you have to lose your temper every time you get upset?"

For once Jo did not hit back at Sally. "It was Holly," she said helplessly. "I kept thinking of her. If I hadn't been bitten by that wretched snake then it would still have been my responsibility to see she was locked up. Instead, it was left to Ross, and he failed."

"Are you so sure about that?"

Jo raised her shoulders and let them fall again. "What else could it be?"

"I doubt if we'll ever know," Sally said, "so it would be better not to toss the blame around without being sure of facts. Holly is dead and it's horrible, but even Sandy is man enough to admit just now that he realised that one day soon Holly would have had to go back where she came from and the same thing could have happened there. Only he added, very wisely, 'In that case we would never have known, would we?' "

When Jo was silent, Sally went on inexorably. "Tell me, Jo—if you don't think much of Ross and I don't think much of Bruce, what do we both think of Neil? Would you trust his judgement, instinctively?"

"Oh, yes," said Jo, walking straight into the neat trap prepared for her.

"He told me earlier on that he thought that Ross Andrews was one of the finest game wardens in Africa. If he failed anywhere it would be because it would be his sense of responsibility was too strong for his own good. He said a lot of other things too, but I won't bore you with them. You might not listen to me. Anyway, that's the man whom you and Bruce Farley are doing your damnedest to denigrate. What he needs is a bit of help with the job he's trying desperately to do, not criticism."

Jo swallowed. Perhaps Sally was right, she was too confused and upset to think straight.

Sally touched her arm. "Come on, Jo, let's go in and have some breakfast. I personally can't do anything constructive on an empty stomach." And as they both turned to go, she added softly, "I had a good evening yesterday. I shall always remember it. You enjoyed yourself too, didn't you?"

157

Jo nodded. She still did not trust herself to speak. In spite of her dislike of crocodiles the evening had been rather special.

"And I'm not going to say it was because Bruce wasn't there," Sally said dryly.

Jo found her voice at last. It came out small and tight. "There's something you ought to know, Sal. Even if I ever admit to being mistaken about Ross Andrews, that still doesn't alter the way I feel about Bruce."

"I didn't expect it to," Sally replied. "I just wanted to know where we stood, that's all."

Jo tore her mind away from her own problems and said impulsively, "You like Neil, don't you?"

"Yes," answered Sally, and her cheeks were faintly pink, "I've never met anyone quite like him before."

They came in to find both Ross and Neil in the sitting room, gulping down a cup of coffee and snatching a bite of breakfast.

"What is it?" said Sally. "Has something else gone wrong?"

"You could say that the day hasn't started well." Ross yelled for one of the boys and told Saku to find Tau, and be damned sure there was plenty of petrol in the truck.

Sally waited. She had learned that Ross would tell them in his own good time.

"I've just had a message from the ranger over on the eastern border to say that he thinks that the only water-hole in operation there has been poisoned. It seems," he added, glancing from Sally to Jo, "that I'm not looking after your interests very well after all."

CHAPTER ELEVEN

"POISONED water-hole?" Jo repeated foolishly, not quite understanding. "What does that mean?"

"By my reading," he said in a tired voice, drained of emotion, "someone has chucked something unpleasant in the last few inches of water over there. The water will be death to drink, so we'll probably lose all the game in that area that can't move fast enough to either the river or fresh water. Or unless it rains. Unfortunately the eastern border is most vulnerable, because it's just about the most widely spaced hole on the reserve.

"Ah, Neil," he turned in relief as his friend returned, "I'm glad you're around. We're in trouble." And he explained with the minimum of words what had happened. "I'm going over there immediately. Do you feel like coming?"

"Of course. I'm ready now, except for collecting my gun. Would it help to use my truck? It's only just had a service, so it may be in better shape than yours."

"Anything is in better shape than ours," Ross said wryly, "but it might be a good idea. It will leave ours free for Kari if he needs it. Unfortunately he's off on a regular twenty-four-hour check-up; probably won't be back until later this morning." He turned to the girls and spoke brusquely.

"Tell him exactly what's happened when he comes. It's the Koanaka hole. It seems fairly certain that if this is serious, then the same band of poachers who've been troubling us recently are responsible for this. There's even a remote chance he's seen something of them, because he's been travelling in an easterly direction. If he's got any idea at all of tracking them, tell him to

159

take anyone he can and go off in the truck. But no rough stuff," he warned, "they'll be armed and probably four or five of them. I just want to get them off the reserve before they can do any more damage. Understood?

Both Sally and Jo nodded.

"Is . . . is there anything at all we can do?" Sally asked.

"No, thanks, just keep an eye on Sandy and on the radio telephone. There's an unusual amount of static on it. Oh, and you could ask Saku to pack up some food."

But Saku needed no telling for a job like that. Food was all ready by the time Neil had filled his own truck with petrol.

They went outside to watch the men leave. Tau was in the back of the truck and Goldie stood beside Jo. The lion seemed uneasy and made little whimpering noises as she watched Ross leave, almost as if she knew her beloved master was driving into trouble.

Neil started up the engine. "Take care!" Sally called. Both men turned and smiled and waved at her.

Jo said nothing to Ross, but after he had gone she half-wished she had. His face was a tight mask of anxiety.

"It's times like these," Sally said slowly after they had gone, "that you realise how helpless we are and the absolute value of men like Neil and Ross."

"Neil, yes," Jo said sharply, "but I'm not so sure about Ross. It was he who said he had let us down, not us. Perhaps he was right."

"Oh, Jo, now you're being ridiculous; you saw how he looked, what on earth do you think he could have done to prevent something like this? The only thing we can hope for is that there's been some genuine mistake and the water-hole isn't poisoned after all. How on earth would Africans poison it, anyway?"

"With all the odd things growing in the bush," Jo pointed out. "How do you think the Bushmen poison the tips of their arrows? There must be dozens of concoctions in a vast country like this."

"Well, apart from that, let's get one thing clear Jo—if, when they come back and there has been real trouble, just let me see you even hint that the blame may lie with Ross and I swear I'll see that you never get a pennyworth of Nyala!"

Jo stared at her gentle, easy-going sister. "You really must be joking."

"I've never been more serious in my life."

Without thinking what she was saying, Jo snapped: "Isn't it time you made up your mind which of those two you're hanging your shirt on?" She stalked off to find Bruce before she could see the whiteness of her sister's face.

Bruce was cleaning the points of his truck. He looked up as she came down the slope to the river.

"Well, darling, I'm sorry to desert you like that, but I thought there were enough people crying over the loss of one pet fawn."

For a second she didn't know what he was talking about. What had happened since had pushed the tragedy of Holly out of her mind.

"I suppose," he added, "your friend Ross had left the cage door open."

"Perhaps, but I doubt if we'll ever really know. Anyway, there's been more trouble to take our minds off Holly." And she told him about the water-hole.

Bruce stood up and stretched his big frame, then wiped his oily hands on a rag. "That sounds like one more nail in the coffin of your friend Andrews."

"What . . . what do you mean?" she said quickly.

"On an efficiently run reserve that kind of thing simply doesn't happen. That's why you have a staff of native rangers, to prevent troubles like that. Something must be wrong somewhere in this set-up, and while Andrews obviously didn't do it himself he has to be held responsible, just like in any business. You know, Jo," he added, seeing her worried face, "with just a few more 'accidents' like this what little stake you have in Nyala will slip right away."

She was silent for a moment, then, as if trying to prove a point to herself, she said, "Neil said he was a very good game warden."

"Jo, my love, Neil Brand is a very good man and like all good men he believes the best of everyone. Andrews is his friend, isn't he? Look, I'm not saying he doesn't know anything about animals, game in general, but that's a far cry from being wholly responsible for an area the size of . . . well, your own county at home."

Again Jo was silent. She suddenly felt very low in spirit, and the need to get away from Nyala, away from Sally and all her disapproval, was stronger than anything.

She said at last : "Will you be staying here today, Bruce?"

"No, I'm going to the site, leaving shortly. I'm just getting to an interesting point there. Today may even prove whether it's worth my mounting a decent sized operation." Her face fell so much that he added casually, "I suppose it's no good asking whether you'd like to come along too? I'll be back around dark tonight."

Her face lit up with joy. He bent down and kissed her. "You're a marvellous girl, Jo, you don't try and hide your feelings. I like that." He glanced down at his watch. "If you could be ready in twenty minutes, we'll make a start then."

Sally was angry when she told her. Sandy also looked disappointed, but she noticed he did not ask to come. He was still influenced in this general feeling against Bruce.

He followed her down the verandah steps where she was putting on stronger shoes a few minutes later. He watched her for a long time before saying suddenly, "I asked my dad if you might marry Mr. Farley. He said you could if you wanted to. You're not going to, Jo, are you?"

"I don't know, Sandy," she replied honestly. "I like Mr. Farley very much, we haven't talked about getting married yet."

"Well, I jolly well hope you don't," he said fiercely.

Jo was puzzled by his attitude. "You mustn't say things like that, Sandy. Mr. Farley is a very nice man. Besides, you didn't feel like this about him when you first came over, or when he drove you over here from home."

"That was before your snakebite," he pointed out.

"Look, Sandy," she said gently, "you think he acted wrongly about my bite—well, I honestly don't know, but you can't go through your life disliking people because they do one thing you disapprove of. Everyone makes mistakes."

"It's not just that," he retorted. "He doesn't like Ross, and anyone who doesn't like Ross is my enemy. And I don't like the way he talks to Kari and Saku and his own Africans. Dad and Ross wouldn't say the things he does."

Jo had no answer to that because she did not know what he meant. It was time, she decided, to end this conversation. She went inside and told Sally what she was doing, reminding her unnecessarily to pass all the messages on to Kari.

"That's something I'm not likely to forget," Sally said in a chilly, un-Sally-like voice.

"I suppose you think I should stay here."

Sally sighed. "Probably, but today it's better that you're out of my sight. One of us will say something more we'll regret."

Jo's spirits began to lift from the moment the house disappeared behind the morning haze. It seemed hotter than ever and Bruce had warned her that his site did not have very much shade, but that it was not too far from a tiny branch of the river.

They reached the area after about an hour and a half, driving through a part of the reserve Jo had not seen before. There seemed little game, apart from small groups of buck, in this part, but more than likely what there was was taking refuge from the heat.

He had chosen an open area, with just a small group of trees under which his two African workers had built a rough shelter and a small cooking fire.

She watched, fascinated, during the next hour while they dug a deep square pit from which Bruce extracted the sand and gravel, washed it in one of the open drums of water that the men had brought from the river, sieved it, then finally turned the sieve upside down on the makeshift sorting table.

He explained to her : "If there were diamond here it would come to the top in this way, because it's heavier than the rest of the gravel."

"I suppose you haven't found anything yet?" she asked, picking over the fine material with her fingers, enjoying the cool wet feeling of the gravel, wishing she could be the one to make the first strike.

"No, I'm a long way from that, but I have found some interesting minerals, which are just the kind that would have been washed down the river with diamonds thousands of years ago."

"But there's no river where you're digging?" she remarked.

"I know, but this is where the expertise comes in. I'm gambling on the fact of this area once—oh, hundreds of years ago—having been the course of the river. I spent the first two days here surveying, after hours over at Neil's place studying the map. Geologically it's possible.

These rivers generally changed their course over the thousands of years."

As the day wore on Jo found it too hot to remain near where Bruce was working with the minimum of shade. He seemed impervious to the heat, but she went over to the shelter of the trees. But even here, she reckoned the temperature must be well over a hundred. She sat back and wondered idly how far away Ross and Neil were, whether their worst fears had been founded.

As usual she had spoken too impulsively to Sally this morning. She loathed quarrelling with her sister. Perhaps both she and Bruce were judging Ross too harshly. Certainly she never found herself looking for the best in him, only the worst.

Very strongly an unbidden picture of him came into her mind. That taut, worried expression masking all his other feelings. Perhaps he did care deeply about Nyala, after all. Perhaps he missed Uncle Harold more than they realised. Perhaps... but she closed her eyes, not wanting to think about Ross Andrews. He was too disturbing a man.

From above her Bruce spoke. "Time for a break, darling. And you look desperately worried. What's wrong?"

But this time she shook her head, not wanting to confide in him. Instead she reached out her hand and let it rest in his. "I wish," he said softly, pushing a damp strand of hair away from her forehead, "I could always look up from my digging or washing and see you sitting there."

He sat down beside her and poured her a glass of lemon from the flask that already seemed too hot to hold. "You know, Jo, you and I could do wonderful things together, even with this place. When you and Sally own it, which by God, I'm going to make sure you do, there's nothing you won't be able to do with it. Let's drink to that day, Jo darling, even in tepid lemonade."

But she paused, guilty suddenly that she had not after all taken him completely into her confidence.

"Bruce . . ."

"Yes, darling?" He bent and kissed her and she clung to him, as though afraid he might vanish once again.

"There's something I haven't told you."

"A secret?"

"No . . . or rather it's something Sally and I decided to keep to ourselves. Our plans for the future. You see, Nyala can never really be ours."

He drew away from her, frowning. "You mean you don't think it's possible to make it pay? Well, I . . ."

"No, not that, although I do think we have only a small chance. No, if we do prove we can manage, then as soon as Nyala becomes ours, or rather Sally and Alan's, then we're committed to selling it. That's the only reason why we came out here. I never dreamed I would fall in love with Nyala," she said sadly.

He gripped her with both arms and for a moment his anger was quite frightening. "Sell it? Sell Nyala? Jo, you must be out of your mind! Who's been getting at you—Sally?"

"No, no, of course not. Please, Bruce, you're hurting me. I'll tell you why, only you must try to understand."

"Go on," he said ominously.

"Well, it's Alan, really. He sacrificed so much for Sally and myself. He's had his heart set on one dream for years now. He wants to buy a small hotel right on the edge of the moor called the Crag Inn. Oh, it's a marvellous place; in an English way, very wild and beautiful. Now it's up for sale for the first time and he thinks he could get first option, because the old ladies who own it have a soft spot for him. Unfortunately, he hasn't a hope of raising the money, even half of it. But with Nyala, this is one way Sally and I can help him."

Bruce raised his hands and let them fall helplessly. "So

you would let all this go for a...a whim of your brother's?"

"It's not a whim, Bruce, and I told you I have no choice. Alan is my brother; I suppose a very special kind of brother. And while it will break my heart to part with Nyala, unless I won the pools or a premium bond or something, nothing would make me change my mind. In any case the final decision would rest with Sally. I couldn't fight against that."

His eyes were closed as if in pain. She had seen Bruce briefly angry, but mostly his big square face was full of laughter. She had never seen him like this. And why? In some ways his concern was curiously misplaced.

"And to think," he said despairingly, "to think what I wanted to do for you, what I did for you..."

"What do you mean?" She stared at him.

But she was not going to find out that day. There was a sudden flurry of movement from the centre of the site. The two Africans working there suddenly put down their spades. They seemed to be jabbering excitedly and as Bruce strained his eyes and muttered, "What the hell's wrong with them now?" they both started to run, right over to the distant thorn trees.

With one accord Bruce and Jo stood up.

"There's someone over there," Jo said sharply. "It's not an animal, it's a man."

"An African," Bruce said after a few moments. "One of their pals, no doubt. If they don't get back to work in ten minutes, I'll dock them an hour's pay."

But Jo was not listening, only staring. "It may be an African, Bruce, but there's something wrong with him—see the way they're pulling him along. Please, we must take the truck along and see if we can do anything."

"As you wish." He got up grudgingly and walked across to the truck.

A few minutes later he drew up in a cloud of dust,

where his two workers were supporting the other man. His leg was bleeding and almost useless, while his dark face was a mask of sweat and pain.

"Oh, Bruce," she cried, "it's the one we call Kwane, Kari's assistant. Please find out what happened. He can hardly speak any English."

For the next few moments Bruce and Kwane jabbered away, each only half understanding the other. The man could not stand, so Jo persuaded him into the passenger seat of the truck. He leaned back against the seat, physically near the end of his tether.

"Bruce, what is it, please tell me," she pleaded.

"As far as I can understand some poachers had a pot shot at him and Kari's gone off after them."

The man's hunted eyes looked from one to the other. "No, no, Kari sick. Very hurt. Find Kari."

"There, you see," she flung at him,. "there is something seriously wrong. Kari's hurt!"

"The fellow's dramatising things. Good God, Kari's a Bushman, he can find his way out of anything."

"Not if he's shot like this man," she snapped. "We've got to get him back to the house and then send out some help."

"Look, Jo, you're a babe in arms as far as this country is concerned. These men are used to far tougher hazards than this. I can't afford to go haring back when all he needs is some clean water and disinfectant, both of which I have. Come on, we'll get the truck back in the shade."

"And Kari?" she said tightly.

"I've told you, he's an African. He's well able to take care of himself."

They reached the trees and he handed her the first aid box and some spare drinking water. She did not trust herself to speak.

He smiled down at her. "Take that martyred expression off your face, Jo, it doesn't suit you. You can't put the wrongs of all the natives to rights, there are other more important things."

"Like diamonds?"

He shrugged. "For the moment, yes. I'll go down and finish up as quickly as I can. A couple of hours and then we'll be on our way."

But as she started to clean up the man's wound, something she had never done before, she realised immediately that a couple of hours would be much too long. The bullet was probably still in there. She soaked a dressing in antiseptic and bandaged it on rather clumsily. She then gave the man a tot of brandy. It was probably the wrong thing to do, but he looked simply terrible.

Then she hesitated, staring across at where Bruce was engrossed again. But of course there was no real choice. If she was going to be able to live with herself there was only one thing to do.

She placed half the supply of drinking water in the shade and most of the carefully wrapped food. She then climbed back into the truck, switched on the engine and, without a backward glance, drove off in the direction in which they had come.

She thought she heard Bruce call out, but still she did not look. Her only fear was that she could not find the way. She thought the man beside her had lost consciousness.

At first there was only one track, but after a few miles it divided and she had to slow down, faced with her first decision. Kwahe opened his eyes and pointed a feeble hand to the right. She breathed again. In that way they reached the house in under two hours.

Within five minutes Saku and the only other boy in the house had lifted Kwane from the truck and on to the cool of the verandah. Sally came out and took the dressing off the wound. The only question she asked was: "Where's Bruce?"

"He . . . he wouldn't come." While Sally went indoors to investigate the main first aid kit Jo turned anxiously to Saku.

"Please, Saku, before he loses consciousness again, you must ask him about Kari. I think Kari is in some kind of trouble, but I can't understand what."

The two men conversed in undertones. Finally Saku stood up slowly, his face torn with emotion. "Lady," he said, "some poachers ambushed the Land Rover. They dragged Kari off with them and when he," he nodded towards the sick man, "tried to help they shot him. They do not like Kari, because they say he is Bushman gone white. This man fears they will do something bad to him. He also said Kari knew how the water-hole was poisoned. He was off to tell the *Morena*."

"The same poachers, of course."

Saku shook his wise old head slowly. "No, he said it was a white man. A bad white man who cares more for the white glass than the animals."

"White glass?" she repeated. "What can he mean?"

"Diamonds, lady. Diamonds."

Her heart seemed to kick with a sickening thud. Kwane was delirious. Even a simple black man had been turned against Bruce. She stood up quickly. "The only important thing is to help Kari, and for that we need Ross and Neil."

From behind her Sally said, "I'm afraid we're in more trouble. The radio telephone is so thick with static I can't raise anyone."

"Not Ross?"

"No, nor the doctor."

"There will be a storm," Saku said flatly.

Jo looked up at the brassy sky and thought he was dreaming. But Bushmen were supposed to know these things, weren't they? They would smell rain hundreds of miles away.

Jo turned to Sally. "Can you cope with Kwane?"

"I don't know. I'll have to try. My first aid knowledge is rather limited."

"Well, it's better than mine. There's only one thing I can do, Sal—drive over to the eastern post and find Ross."

Sally nodded. "Yes, you'll have to. I'll keep trying the radio telephone."

Within minutes Saku had produced a map of the reserve. She prayed fervently she would be able to follow it. With that, and Saku's excellent directions, she reckoned she had a good chance.

She went out to the truck. The engine caught, then coughed and died. Ten minutes later there was still not even a spark of life.

"Can you . . ." she started towards Saku.

He shook his head mutely.

She swallowed. There was only one way open to her now. Briskly she gave her next orders. "Saddle Brandy for me, Saku, and you'd better put everything in the saddlebags you would put for the *Morena*, including a gun."

Sally caught at her arm. "You're mad, Jo, you can't go all that way on a horse. If you don't get lost you'll have no protection from . . . from anything."

"So you're suggesting I leave Kari to die, because I'm a bit scared? Look, Ross has told me that the most dangerous thing on horseback is camel-thorn. Added to which it's still the hot part of the day, so there won't be much game around."

"And the gun? You've only tried it a few times."

"It's to fire when I get near to the post."

"Please, Jo . . . if you got lost."

"I won't. Besides, Saku says it's one of the easiest trails to follow in the park. Even he thinks I can manage it."

When Saku came to tell her that Brandy was ready and saddled, she kissed Sally quickly and said, "Don't worry about me, it's ... it's just another adventure. And, Sal, I'm sorry about saying those things to you. Perhaps you're right about Bruce, I don't know. At the moment I can hardly bear to think about him."

Saku shook her gravely by the hand. "You are a very brave lady. *Morena* will be very proud of you."

"That's something, I suppose," said Jo dryly. She kicked her heels into Brandy's flank and rode off towards the lonely desert.

CHAPTER TWELVE

JO had been riding for just over two hours. She had stopped only once for a drink of the now warm water she carried in a large metal flask. At first she had been very hot indeed, but at last she appeared to have found her second wind and the heat was no more than mere discomfort. She felt she had temporarily come to terms with it.

She had also been rather frightened when she turned round and could no longer see the familiar landmarks. Now even those fears had been overcome, or perhaps merely suppressed, although not her watchfulness. It was one of the things both Ross and Kari had drummed into her, that once you were no longer frightened of the bush then it was easy to get careless. Just like that first time she rode out.

Actually she had seen little but the friendlier kind of game; a herd of zebra, plenty of impala and other buck. Once when she stopped, a hyena stared at her from the undergrowth and in the distance she had seen a pack of wild dogs. She had also heard the trumpeting of elephants, and only then did she feel the need to urge Brandy forward, but when she realised the sound came from the west, probably a mile or more away, her heartbeat steadied again.

She had consulted the map several times, but once they were well on the trail she realised Brandy knew by instinct where they were going. With luck she should be within firing distance in another hour. She hoped so fervently, glancing up at the sky. Of one thing she would be very, very frightened indeed; spending a night in the bush alone. Strange, the sound of thunder had never been very far away, although rain appeared an impossibility.

Until now she had concentrated on her journey. It had seemed very important to do that for her own safety. But there was another reason, of course. She did not want to think about Bruce.

She would not allow herself to think of the implications of what Kwane had said. She simply did not believe it. But right deep lingered the faintest suspicion of doubt. Bruce had callously abandoned a man because he was black—no, two men, if you counted Kari. It had not occurred to him that these two men were more important than his own work—just for a single day. The discovery of this side of his character had numbed Jo until now. Could she really love a man who had no room in his heart at all for his fellow men? She thought about the others' reactions to Bruce. Both Sally and Ross had instinctively been against him. Had they seen a darker side of his character much earlier? Then there was young Sandy. They say a child instinctively judges another human being. Well, certainly Sandy knew his own mind. *Oh, Bruce, Bruce, can I really love you one minute and doubt you so dreadfully the next?*

There was something else that only now came to the surface of her mind; his anger that she and Sally intended to sell Nyala, if it became theirs. He obviously had not understood that however much you hated the result you could not go back on your word. But why had *he* been so angry? Nyala was nothing to him. Even if he found diamonds he would still reap the rewards. Or was she the way to a personal stake in Nyala?

Her sickness at even the thought of such a ruthless betrayal had made her jerk Brandy to a halt. No, not that, *never, never, never.*

"Get out of my mind, Bruce," she said aloud. She would talk to him later. For the moment she must put all her energies into finding Kari. She dug her heels into Brandy's flanks and he responded instinctively.

Just under an hour later she saw in the far distance a clump of trees, the first she had seen for a long time. It must be the post. She drew the gun from its saddle holster and fired three times into the air. Five minutes later she saw the cloud of dust that could only mean the truck was on its way.

She patted Brandy's smooth neck, now wet with sweat. "Thanks," she whispered. "One thing, Ross was quite right about you. You're a truly faithful friend."

With a squeal of tyres the truck stopped and Ross jumped out.

"My God, Jo, you must be mad! No ... no, something must be wrong. Here, let me help you down."

"For once," she said shakily, "I think I need help. I'm practically glued in the same position."

He almost lifted her from the saddle, then gently led her to the truck. "You can talk in a moment, when we get back." He patted Brandy's rump, pointed in the direction of the post and said, "There, off you go." The horse trotted off and was soon a small cloud of dust.

The post was little more than a wooden hut set amongst the trees, but there was a chair, some blessed shade and reasonably cool water. The two Africans there seemed amazed that a woman had ridden so far, and Neil thoughtfully produced a bowl of water and a sponge to cool her face and hands.

"Now," said Ross, "if you feel up to it, tell me."

So she started from the moment Kwane had appeared at the edge of the prospecting site to the point where the truck wouldn't start.

Neil was immediately puzzled. "But surely Bruce could have fixed the truck? It was surely something minor since the thing had been well looked after."

"I ... I drove from the site alone, with Kwane."

"You mean he wouldn't come?" Neil was incredulous.

She could not bring herself to answer.

"Right," said Ross, carrying on quickly, "you say Kwane told you this story about Kari. But have you any idea where they were when the poachers appeared?"

She nodded, pulling the map from her pocket. "I marked the place where the Land Rover was last left. Saku explained to me what Kwane had told him."

"Good girl!"

"A girl in a million, I'd say," Neil said, and Ross looked down at her with an odd expression. For just a brief second his hand rested on her shoulder.

"Right," he went on, "they say troubles never come singly. We must take the truck and find Kari just as soon as we can. I don't like the sound of this at all. The trouble is I daren't take either of the boys with me, Neil. It would leave this place wide open."

"I daresay you and I can cope," Neil said quietly, "but it might be a longish job."

It was Jo's turn to make an observation. "I don't think we can leave Nyala just like that with no one there and the radio telephone out of order. To start with I'm sure that Kwane needs real medical help, much more than Sally can give. Then . . . then there's Bruce. He's stuck out in the bush with no means of transport, no means of communication. But Kwane comes first," she added quickly.

The two men looked at each other. "I suppose," said Neil, "I could ride back, once Brandy is rested. Taking the short cuts the truck can't manage I should be there in less than three hours."

"There are only two hours to darkness," Ross pointed out.

"At that point Brandy can get me home blindfold. I think probably Jo is right. If I can get the truck going I can come out and help. You'll also need more petrol. The only thing is—Jo."

"She could stay here."

Jo looked about her. She never was very good at merely waiting. "I'm going with Ross," she said clearly. "Another pair of eyes and hands might be useful."

"But you've been riding for four hours," Ross protested. "You must be exhausted."

"I must admit to a sore behind, but as long as you don't put me on a horse again... And if there's any chance of a real wash and something to eat I'll be as good as new." It was almost the truth at that moment. Or was she trying to prove herself to Ross?

While the men made all the other preparations she was shown to a primitive outhouse where a bucket was rigged up as a kind of shower. She even managed to wash her thin cotton blouse of its layer of dust, reckoning it would be dry by the time it came to leave.

With her hair wet and shining, her body blissfully cool, wrapped in a rough sheet, she came back to the hut and tucked into the tin of corned beef, the can of beer and bowl of fresh fruit. By the time that was over she truly felt a different person, apart from the general soreness of body.

About an hour after she first arrived Ross was leading the way out to the truck. Neil had already left, having made sure Brandy had had some food and water, a good rub down and as long a rest as possible.

Jo had watched them leave. "Will Brandy be able to make it?" she asked anxiously.

Ross nodded. "Brandy's a very tough horse, used to intense heat and rough terrain. Also he hasn't been galloped to a standstill. He'll be tired, but Neil won't drive him hard."

Just about an hour after they left the post they found the abandoned truck tilted at an angle off the track. Although the windscreen was smashed it seemed otherwise undamaged.

Ross peered in. "I should think Kari managed to get

rid of the ignition key. That would be his first thought; to immobilise the truck."

He stood, a taut, lonely figure in the gathering darkness of the bush, examining the ground for any kind of track. Jo tried to make herself useful by starting a search for the key, but it was a hopeless job.

After a while he said, "They're heading north-west. Why, I wonder? There's hardly a thing over there. I don't like the look of it at all. But I'm going to find Kari. I've got to," he added fiercely. "Kari is a man who would give his life for a friend."

Jo came to stand beside him. "Can you do anything tonight?"

"No, we would only lose them. I'm afraid it's a question of resting until first light. Do you think you can take it?"

"Of course."

"Yes, that was a foolish question to ask. You've already shown that. You've made your own sacrifice for Kari. That was the kind of decision back at the prospecting site no girl should be asked to take."

"Was it?" she said in a muffled voice, turning away from him. "I imagine anyone would have done the same thing."

"Perhaps. Perhaps not. Not when it could change the course of your life."

Suddenly, with the depth of his understanding, all her resolve broke. She was tired, drained of feeling and she had been dry-eyed for too long. She sank down on to the sand and wept.

For a few moments he let her cry. He knew she needed to cry. Then he put a glass into her hand and ordered her to drink.

She gulped down the brandy and stared at him, tortured, hardly knowing who he was. "He didn't care," she sobbed, "he didn't care that they were both human beings and there was no one else to help.

Kwane could have died. Kari might be dead already. You can't love someone like that, can you?"

"Love can withstand many tests, I imagine," he said quietly, "but once it's shaken to its very roots, then there's no going back. I learned that a long time ago. But *did* you really love him, Jo?"

She shook her head from side to side. "Now, I don't know. I only know I thought I did. And there's something else you don't know. Kwane told us that Kari knew who had poisoned your water-hole. A white man; a man seeking diamonds. I kept telling myself that he must be wrong. Why should Bruce want to do a thing like that?"

"I can't answer that, Jo. I hope, I really hope it isn't true."

"If it were true," she said dully, "he wouldn't want Kari found, would he?"

He took hold of both her shoulders and raised her to her feet.

"I don't know that either. I only know that we both have a job to do and we're both determined to do it. First we're going to make a fire. I want you to find me as much dry thorn and brush as you can—small stuff and big stuff. It's something we have to keep going all night. Then you're going to make some coffee and we'll have a snack before we sleep. I want to check over the truck so that we're quite ready to leave by dawn."

She was glad of things to do, and though she was tired, it was better than sitting doing nothing. By the time the fire was going and the coffee prepared he had run the engine sweetly and pulled out the seats of one truck to make her a bed in the back of the other. For himself there was a rug and pillow on the ground near the fire.

She looked uncertain. "Will . . . will you be all right?"

"Fine." He grinned for the first time that evening,

the firelight etching the sharp bones of his face. "I'm used to it, and anyway there's not enough flesh on me to make a good eating proposition."

Afterwards they cleared up and then he helped her up to the back. "Sleep well, Jo," he said softly, "remember your first night under the stars. The great thing about unhappiness is that it never lasts."

"I've tried to make you unhappy, though, haven't I?"

"No, because you never really meant it."

"But I did," she cried passionately, "I've been abominable to you right from the beginning. I should have trusted you, but I always act before I think. And I listened to Bruce, too."

"Look, Jo," he reached in and covered her hand resting on the side. "Look, Jo, if there's any blame, then it must lie equally with me. I never wanted you or Sally, or anyone, to come and disturb my particular paradise. I'm intolerant, I know I am. That's probably why the girl I was going to marry walked out on me. I could never imagine that anyone could feel about Nyala the way I do. I saw it all changing and I didn't want change. I merely deceived myself."

"No, we deceived you as well, Sally and I. Since I want there to be no misunderstanding from now on I have to tell the other thing that will turn you right against us all over again."

He laughed very quietly. "You mean that if Nyala is yours you intended to sell it!"

She gaped at him. "But how did you *know*?"

"I didn't know, I guessed; it seemed so obvious. Then I asked Sally. I knew she couldn't lie. I understand why you are trying to do it. At least it's an honourable reason."

"Bruce didn't. But then Bruce wanted Nyala for himself, didn't he?" She asked the question quite calmly.

His lack of response was answer enough. After all, she was the only one who had not seen through him.

"I'm glad you told me now, about the selling. I kept telling myself that you would, in your own good time. Sally said you were too honest a person for your own good. Now go to sleep, Jo, we have a lot to face tomorrow."

"All right. And Ross—"

"Yes?"

"Thanks." She bent forward and kissed him impulsively.

Jo woke to the rumble of thunder and lay for a moment trying to get her bearings. She had slept soundly from the moment she put her head on the makeshift pillow.

Now there were other sounds in the darkness, the crackle of a fire newly stirred into life and clink of metal cups. She peered out to find Ross bending over the coffee pot, outlined in the flames. She combed her hair and pulled on her blouse, then jumped down to join him.

"Sleep well?" he asked.

"Yes, marvellously. I'm still a bit stiff, but otherwise ready for anything." She glanced down at the fire. "Good heavens, ham and eggs? It seems almost too civilised, but it smells out of this world."

"With the sort of day ahead of us that I envisage, we shall need something inside us. Dawn will be breaking in less than half an hour. We must be ready to leave at just that moment."

She thought of Kari and it was no longer just an adventure. "What hopes do you really think we have, Ross?"

"I don't like to estimate things like that." He cocked his ear at another rumble of thunder. "That's the thing that worries me. We want rain more than anything else, yet if it does rain every track will be wiped out and we won't have a hope in hell of finding him. But thunder can roll around the skies for days here before a sign of rain."

"Saku said it was going to rain," she said, suddenly remembering.

"Then you may be sure it is. That's Bushman lore."

They ate their breakfast in companionable silence, then, as Jo started to clear up, he said, "I want to tell you something, Jo. From now on my whole effort is being concentrated on finding Kari. If I appear to be unsympathetic to your tiredness, or drive you on when you want to stop, that's the only reason."

"I know," she nodded. "I only hope I'm as tough as I think I am!"

As the first pale streaks of dawn crossed the sky, Ross started the truck and they were driving into the desert. He had left a note for Neil on their general direction, but that was all they could do.

For an hour he drove on steadily, stopping every now and then to examine the tracks. At the end of that time she said, "I know I can manage this for a time. It would be better if I drove and you gave all your attention to the track."

Without a word he nodded and changed places with her.

It was nearly four hours before he called a fifteen-minute halt, to cool the engine and have a drink. She was already aching with tiredness and she could feel the beginnings of blisters on her hands from having to grip the heavy steering wheel against the force of the rough terrain. But nothing would have drawn a complaint from her.

They had a fresh orange each and he made her take a glucose tablet. The heat was like a dull interminable ache all about her. She wanted to ask him about their progress, but knew he would tell her when he thought it necessary. She turned and found his eyes resting thoughtfully on her.

"I have a problem," he said. "It concerns you."

"Yes?" She waited.

"If we drive on for more than another few miles we shan't have enough petrol to get us back. Now do we carry on until we run out and hope that Neil will have followed the trail I've laid, or do we drive to the only clump of trees I know for about five miles, leave the truck hidden and walk?"

"I imagine you would prefer to walk, wouldn't you?" she said with more calmness than she felt.

He smiled, and for a moment he looked happy. "You're learning, Jo Fraser, you're learning fast. We'll make a good bushwoman out of you yet. I could leave you in the truck, of course."

She did not even bother to answer that one, but climbed back into the driving seat, waiting for him to close the passenger door.

They reached Ross's hiding place and camouflaged the truck as best they could. At least now it could only be seen about twenty yards away. In a canvas bag slung over his shoulder he packed some food, as much water as they could carry and a few essential medical supplies. The only other thing he needed was his gun.

Jo had not given the matter of actually walking in the bush...or rather desert now...any serious thought. It was just as well, she considered some time later, or she would probably never have left the security of the truck.

There was practically no shade and the sand made walking both difficult and tiring. Worst of all was the heat, dry, gritty and utterly unrelenting. Jo walked behind Ross because it was easier following his footsteps than finding her own. She was like an automaton incapable of any thought but covering the ground. She did wonder how far they would be expected to walk, for with every step forward there was one to retrace. All the time the thunder rumbled overhead and while she longed for the blessed release of rain, she knew that was one thing she must not pray for—yet.

Ross turned and smiled encouragement at her, but he never spoke. He never changed his step except once, when he stopped abruptly and put his arm out so that she stumbled against it. She saw the tiny black snake slither away into the sand.

They had not seen any game since they started walking. It was just as well, Jo thought, she could not move any faster than she was going now.

Then Ross stopped again. This time he knelt to examine marks on the ground. Even she could see that it looked like a disturbance in the sand. For the first time she asked him a direct question. "It is human, isn't it?"

He nodded. "If I'm wrong, then we can't go much further. There's nothing but desolation ahead and no human could survive out there. We shall have to turn back and wait for Neil." He cupped his hands round his mouth and called, a strange high-pitched sound that was like one animal calling another.

At first there was nothing. The silence and desolation was complete. Then Ross called again.

Jo lifted her head sharply, wakened at last out of her stupor. The sound was so small that it could have been nothing. But Ross had heard it and he jerked his head at her to follow him. From somewhere she found the energy to keep up with his increased stride.

It was another fifteen minutes before they found Kari. Jo barely smothered the gasp of horror. He was bound hand and feet to a thorn tree and he sagged against his bonds. His back was a mass of scratches from the terrible thorns and his face almost drained of life.

While Jo hacked him loose Ross got the first few

drops of water down his throat. He opened his eyes and in a queer cracked voice said, "I knew you would come, *Morena*."

Together they eased him to the ground and Ross cradled him in his arms, taking the pressure off that dreadful back, tipping more water drop by drop into the dry, swollen throat.

Ross asked him only one question. "How long, Kari?"

"Yesterday afternoon," came the whispered answer.

"Will he be all right?" Jo asked.

"I think so. I hope so. Bushmen have a strong sense of survival. What I don't understand is why Neil isn't here. He should have caught up by the time we started walking. That's why I didn't want to take the truck farther. I suppose it could be something serious wrong with the truck."

"I don't think so," she said slowly. "It was running perfectly well until I actually arrived back at the house. And I know Bruce was very fussy about its servicing."

"Then we must just walk and hope."

"And Kari?" She looked down at the sick, exhausted man.

"Thank God Bushmen are small."

"You mean you're going to *carry* him?" She was aghast.

"If you can manage bag and gun. I have no choice."

That walk back to the hidden truck was a nightmare. Some of the time Jo felt she was actually sleepwalking. But if she found the conditions unbearable, what of Ross, who would walk for perhaps a quarter of a mile, let down his burden, rest for a few minutes, then start again.

Most of the time Kari was unconscious, but once he woke and begged: "Leave me, *Morena*, please leave me . . . you cannot carry me." But Ross merely put him over his shoulder more firmly and trudged on.

At least when they reached the truck, there was enough water for a long drink and some to sponge their faces and, more important, Kari's back. She watched Ross do it, as gently as if he were handling a child. She felt extraordinarily moved by the sight. She handed him the bottle of antiseptic, feeling tears of relief gather in her throat that they had come through this far together. She knew one thing with complete certainty. There was no other man who could have done what Ross did, no other man who could make her feel so proud or so humble.

There was no question who should drive. Ross would not have had the strength, although he would have died rather than admit it. She did not even wait to be asked, but climbed back into the driving seat.

It was better than walking, but not a great deal, because with passing time the fiery pain in her hands seemed to cloud her thoughts. But at least they were able to go just a little faster. And by the time they reached the other, abandoned truck, at least they were on some kind of track.

Again Ross was puzzled, for there was still no sign of Neil. It could only be that he had had to rush Kwane to medical help.

Nearly twenty-four hours after Jo had set out yesterday she saw the landmark of trees in the distance. Could it really be Nyala, or was it just a mirage? She knew at this point that she was just about at the end of her tether. Ross was still supporting Kari, keeping his back away from pressure, holding him against the continual bumping of the truck.

They were all out in front to greet them, having seen the familiar cloud of dust. Kari was lifted by willing hands of his own friends, and Jo was helped down by Neil and Sally.

Neil said abruptly, "How bad is he?"

"We got him in time. Look at his back, then a

sedative and a long sleep and he'll be all right by morning." Ross looked round. "I suppose you had to use Farley's truck for Kwane?"

"You suppose wrong," Neil replied grimly. "I got it going almost immediately, and since Kwane was holding his own and we'd managed to get a message to the hospital the only time the damned radio telephone functioned I decided I ought to pick up Farley first. He was only an hour or so away. If necessary we could then both drive Kwane towards town." He paused.

"Go on." It was Jo who said that, knowing that the grimness of Neil's expression concerned Bruce in some way.

"On the way back here we had a few . . . words, then I came in to check on Kwane. By the time I came out again he'd driven off and left us all flat."

Jo felt sick. But calmly she said, "Then it must have been true about what Kari had seen him do?"

"I'm afraid so, Jo," Neil said gently. "When I accused him he didn't really know that Kari had seen him. It was enough to scare him off. I should have had the sense to keep my mouth shut. At least we might still have had the truck."

But it was no time for explanations. All Jo wanted was the blissful cool of a shower, clean clothes and something to take the burning pain from her hands.

When she came out of the bathroom Goldie was curled up on her bed as if to welcome her back safely and Sally was waiting with a pot of salve. "Here," she said severely, "give me those hands."

Jo winced, but some of the pain was soothed away almost immediately. She watched her sister for a moment before taking a deep breath.

"I'm sorry, Sal."

"What on earth for?"

"I was wrong about Bruce, and you were right, after all."

"I may not have cared for him much," Sally said soberly, "but I never expected anything like this. Why do you think he put poison in the water-hole? What did he hope to gain?"

"I keep thinking about it," Jo answered, "and I still don't really know, except that he wanted Ross to get the blame for anything that went wrong. He badly wanted us to get rid of Ross. And I was tempted, wasn't I?"

Sally laid a hand on her sister's arm. "Well, the past is past, and if you can try to forget Bruce I think you'll be happier."

Jo shook her head, saying wryly, "I can't forget him, but I promise you every single feeling I had for him was smashed to smithereens. He could have been responsible for the deaths of two men. Kari couldn't have lasted very much longer. And Kwane?"

"He'll be all right. It seems he was mainly suffering from loss of blood, but again he couldn't have survived in the bush with a wound like that. By the way, Jo, I must rub salt in a little more deeply. Neil says he's fairly certain there isn't a hope of diamonds on Nyala. He always thought that Bruce just wanted an excuse to be near you. I think Neil is probably right."

"Of course he is." Jo caught her sister's eye.

Sally gave one of her rare blushes. "Well, I'm not ashamed. It looks possible that I shall be the one to stay out here, not you."

"Oh, Sal, how marvellous!" Jo hugged her sister. "I like him too. I like him very very much. And then of course there's Sandy. We'll both be related to Sandy!"

"Hey, hold on a minute! We haven't really got as far as that. But we both seem to feel exactly the same. I think we knew that first day at lunch. I can't really believe it yet." She glanced down at her watch. "Here, it's time to eat, and then you must go to bed. You must be exhausted after a day like you've had."

"I think I probably am," Jo said, "but I'm hungry too and I want to see how Kari is, and Ross."

Ross was in the living room pouring drinks for them all and answering eager questions from Sandy. He put a glass down beside Jo, then took hold of both her wrists and turned her hands over.

"You drove all that way and you never said a thing." His voice was low.

"I couldn't," she answered with a brave attempt at flippancy, "the chauffeur had gone off duty." She changed the subject swiftly. "Is Kari all right?"

"Yes, he's sleeping. Thanks to you, we got him well in time."

After they had eaten Ross went to check on Brandy, to see how well he had survived the gruelling journey. Jo felt the sudden onset of tiredness, but before she went to bed she decided on a last walk, down to the river, to where Bruce had had his camp.

She looked about her. Apart from the remains of the fire, and the signs that someone had left hurriedly, it was difficult to think that this had been a man's temporary home. She felt no nostalgia, no regrets, nothing at all. It was as though Bruce's actions had cut off at the roots her emotional need for him.

She stood for a moment watching the gentle movements of the river, the way it swirled as it came to a group of rushes and then moved into a pool of calm. The night was warm, but not too hot; impossible to imagine the oven-like temperatures of today's trek.

As she stood up to make her way back to the house and to the welcome thought of a long, long sleep, she became aware of the figure standing against the trees.

"How's Brandy?" she asked softly.

"Like Kari, he's tough." He paused. "I came to tell you how sorry I am about Farley. You must feel very . . . cast adrift."

"Because I came down here?" She looked about her.

"No, it's strange, as I told Sally, after what's happened I can feel nothing, nothing at all. I only came down here to prove it to myself. I'm even beginning to wonder about Holly's death. Perhaps he was even capable of that. I don't know. I don't think, deep down, I could ever have been truly in love with him. I was probably in love with a sort of dream. Anyway, I've awoken from the dream, so don't let's talk about it."

"Shall I tell you something, Jo?" And when he saw her quizzical expression, "I think, like me, you belong to Africa. You have a feeling for it."

She sighed. "I only know I don't want to leave. But tell me something truthfully, Ross, and this time I'll believe you. Do you think we can make Nyala pay on its own?"

"No," he said bluntly. "Oh, with the help of a few small safaris, we can rub along for a little longer, but without real capital I'm afraid it's a lost cause. I mean it when I say I wish from the bottom of my heart it wasn't true, but in two months' time we shall have to face facts. But there is one thing, and now it's my turn to make a confession to you—and Sally—but I'll do that later."

She waited, aware of the tiny grip of fear in her stomach. He was going to leave them after all.

"As you know," he went on, "at the end of three months Nyala—if our attempt fails—has to be handed over to the State. What I have learned, and kept to myself, is that although they make no payment for the actual property, they would have to make an offer for what are loosely called fixtures and fittings—everything that's not the actual game park which your uncle owned. It would work out at something in the region of ten thousand pounds."

"Ten thousand pounds?" she repeated stupidly, "but that's a lot of money! And if," she said with growing excitement, "Alan were to sell the house and add that money—why, he would probably be only about five thousand pounds short. He would cope with that himself with mortgages and things. Oh, do you really think that's so, Ross?"

"Yes, I'm as certain as can be. But what about your house? You and Sally?"

"I don't think Sally will be going home for long, do you? And me—well, the hotel would be my home whenever I wanted it."

"But you're not going home yet, are you?"

"I ... I don't want to. But I think Sally will agree that if all this is so, it's foolish to fight for something you can't win. We must hand Nyala over before it's too late. You would remain warden, wouldn't you?"

"There's a good chance of that. And I'll need help, you know, Jo."

"Not my sort of help?" she said unsteadily.

"Just your sort of help." He took hold of her wrists and looked down at her hands again. "I keep wanting to hold your hands and to thank you for bringing me to my senses."

"Isn't the boot on the other foot?"

"No. I've learned more about myself in the last three weeks than in the past four years. I really believed I wanted to shut myself off from the world. And then you—and Sally—came, and I saw that there were still girls in the world who wanted to give, not take everything. Who really believed in something and were not afraid to speak their minds."

"Sally, yes," she smiled, shaking her head, "everyone knows that about Sally, but not me."

"True, it was easy to see in Sally. Look at Neil—one day and he was lost. But you—you were a challenge, Jo, and all my life I've loved a challenge. And I knew you must be all right," he teased, "when Goldie took to you. She's friendly, but fussy."

Suddenly the thunder that had still been hovering all

the evening rumbled so loudly that it could only have come from overhead. He looked upwards and shouted with joy.

"Jo, look, look, it's a miracle at last! It's going to rain!" And with that the first spots fell and before they had turned and run for the house, the whole skies had opened.

They stood on the verandah, watching, laughing in their delight. And then suddenly he pulled her head towards his shoulder. "It's going to be a good day tomorrow, Jo. It's going to be a good day for both of us."

"Yes," she answered softly, "I rather think it is." Together they turned and went into the house.